Crabbe

Crabbe

WILLIAM BELL

Fitzhenry & Whiteside

Published in Canada by Fitzhenry & Whiteside, 195 Allstate Parkway, Markham,
Ontario L3R 4T8

Published in the United States by Fitzhenry & Whiteside, 311 Washington
Street, Brighton, Massachusetts 02135

www.fitzhenry.ca   godwit@fitzhenry.ca

10 9 8 7 6 5 4 3 2

Library and Archives Canada Cataloguing in Publication

Bell, William, 1945-
        Crabbe / William Bell.
First published: Toronto : Irwin, 1986.
ISBN 1-55005-051-6
        I. Title.
PS8553.E4568C73 2006   jC813'.54   C2005-907261-X

U.S. Publisher Cataloging-in-Publication Data (Library of Congress Standards)

Bell, William, 1945-
        Crabbe / William Bell.
Original U.S. ed: Boston : Little, Brown, 1986.
[160] p. : cm.
Summary: The night before his final exams, a semi-alcoholic teenager packs up
his gear and disappears into the woods. Totally unprepared for bush life, he
nearly dies until he meets someone else who has her own reasons to hide.
ISBN 1-55005-051-6 (pbk.)
1. Runaways — Fiction. 2. Survival — Fiction. 3. Canoes and canoeing —
Fiction. 4. Coming of age — Fiction. 5. Canada – Fiction. I. Title: Crabbe's
journey. II. Title.
[Fic] dc22   PZ7.B41187Cr 2006

Fitzhenry & Whiteside acknowledges with thanks the Canada Council for the
Arts, and the Ontario Arts Council for their support of our publishing program. We
acknowledge the financial support of the Government of Canada for our
publishing activities.

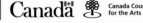 

Design by Fortunato Design Inc., Toronto
Cover art by James Bentley

Printed and bound in Canada

For Megan and Dylan

ST. BARTHOLEMEW'S GENERAL HOSPITAL
TORONTO, ONTARIO

CERTIFICATE OF ADMISSION

DATE: **Nov. 15**

NAME IN FULL: **Franklin Crabbe**

ADDRESS: **not available at this time**

O.H.I.P. NUMBER: **unknown**

PERSON TO BE NOTIFIED: **no name given**

ADDRESS: **not available**

DIAGNOSIS ON ADMISSION:

— **physical exhaustion**

— **pneumonia, both lungs (minor)**

— **injury to left hand: two fingers amputated (see acc. file)**

— **general evidence of exposure**

RECEIVING DR.

COMMENTS:

Patient transferee from Huntington General Hospital after emergency operation left hand: two digits amputated.

Patient admitted ward 4. Further information see file.

Crabbe's Journal: 1

Sometimes at night after they've turned out the lights I sit up in bed and just watch the highway. I prop up the pillows behind me, lean back on the headboard, link my fingers behind my head and sort of drift off. It's a nice, quiet time; there's no noise from the ward except the soft squeak of a nurse's shoes on the floors or maybe a distant cough, and I can let my mind slip through the window out across the frosted lawns and naked shrubs to the road which is lit dimly by amber lamps.

I like to watch the moving lights and listen to the sounds of motion. The cars sift through with a sibilant whoosh, moving fast. It's the trucks I like best though. They power along, lit up with colored lights around the cabs and along the trailers, the big diesels snorting and grinding up the grade.

I suppose I spend a lot of the day watching the highway too. It's pretty boring in this place, especially since they moved me to a private a few days ago. I can always go to one of the wards and get up a game of checkers or cribbage with one of the men but that gets tedious after a while. A lot of them watch T.V. but I don't. There's nobody my age on our floor since I came—all the teenagers are up on Fifth in the psycho ward. I'm in this ward because they don't quite know what to do with me.

The only real point of interest is my daily hour with Dr. Browne. He's the shrink who's got the job of discovering What's Wrong With Crabbe. Until today, I've held him off pretty well—mainly because he's easy to figure and his methods are obvious. As soon as I find out what role he's going to play that day I can put on a corresponding costume and try to keep him under control until the interview is over. Acting sincere helps.

Maybe I should explain. He will always be either Father, Friend or Firm. He doesn't have much faith in honesty, I've discovered. When he's Father he will be all authority and show great paternal concern for me. And he'll control the discussions (if you can call them that) without trying to pretend he isn't. As Friend he's the funniest—though of course I never let on. He tries very hard to get *down* to my level and be a pal, one of the boys. He even takes a few pathetic shots at slang. Only his expressions are from the movies or a thousand years out of date: "What's goin' down today, Franklin?" Last meeting he told me as I left that I probably thought I was a "groovy guy." Can you believe it? I broke up when I heard that one. Luckily I was almost out the door. His nurse gave me a strange look.

Firm is the touchiest for me because then he isn't messing around with textbook methods. He even shows anger at times. I try to steer him off Firm because that's the biggest threat to me. He comes too close then.

So I play the game with him—by my rules. I know it's cynical but I have to do it. It's like he doesn't listen, like he's already decided what you should be saying. I tried to tell him that I don't *want* to talk about what happened, that I just want to be left alone. But, like most adults, he doesn't hear. "Why did you want to die, Crabbe?" he asked me one time. Useless to tell him that I *didn't* want to die. But he kept on, pulling out these bloody obvious shrink tricks like the three F's, circling me like a predator looking for an opening.

Like most grown-ups, he thinks teenagers are basically stupid and easily manipulated. He thinks he can find feeling with an X-ray machine. People my age may not know how to juggle the books or play politics, but feelings we know about.

Last session, for instance, he was Father. He kept me waiting outside his office, as usual. When I went in he was sitting in his customary pose behind his desk. To look at his office you'd swear he never did anything in there all day. Not a thing was out of place. On his large desk top were a phone (black), a brass lamp, a pen, a green blotter with leather edges, and one clean ashtray—all in exactly the same place each day. I did my best to fill up the ashtray with burnt matches.

He always looked the same too: three-piece suit, dark tie, white shirt. Mr. Respectability. He was short and pudgy with fat little fingers and three chins. His heavy horn-rimmed glasses frequently slipped down his nose. He was almost bald but hadn't accepted the fact yet.

In a way, Dr. Browne looked a little like a fat, elementary school kid who somehow managed to sneak into the principal's office and was trying out the chair just for fun. I often wondered if his shoes touched the floor: the chair was one of those high-backed jobs with solid, upholstered arms and he looked lost in it.

On this particular day he was being Father, so my comfy chair was carefully placed a little to the left of center across from him. We made the ritual small-talk that was supposed to break the ice. Was I comfortable? Was the food all right?—stuff like that. Then he started in, but with an indirect approach.

"By the way, Franklin, I've meant to talk to you about your smoking." He crossed his pudgy legs and rested his hands lightly on the chair arms. On his right little finger was a gold signet ring that looked like a collar on a tiny piglet.

I was, at that point, in the middle of filling my pipe, which isn't easy when your left hand is bandaged and has only two fingers and a thumb. I zipped up the tobacco pouch and jammed it into the back pocket of my jeans. I struck a wooden match on the metal zipper of my pants and put it to the bowl, blowing out a cloud of soft blue smoke (the color of smoke you see on a lazy July morning when your campfire is coaxing the chill out of the air). Then I flipped the spent match toward the ashtray—and missed.

The shrink frowned. He reached out and picked up the match between thumb and forefinger handling it like it was a fly dropping, and let it fall into the glass ashtray. He leaned back in his chair, pretending not to be annoyed that the ashtray had been violated.

"Your general health is up to par now," he continued, "owing to the excellent care you've received since you were admitted two weeks ago. But, as we know, Franklin, smoking is injurious to one's health and you are well on your way toward developing a habit that may well prove exceedingly difficult to master."

Plastering on my Concerned Look, I flashed what I hoped would be an innocent smile.

"Oh, don't worry, Fa—, Doctor, I don't inhale the smoke," I almost blew it that time. "And anyway," I said, leaning forward, "I read in the *Science Canada* magazine that pipe smokers develop cancer eighty-seven point nine percent less than cigarette smokers."

This was a lie, but I figured he couldn't have read *every* magazine in the world. I thought the "point nine" was a nice touch.

"Anyway," I hurried on, "I like smoking—enough to balance the risk, that's for sure. How do you like the aroma of this tobacco?"

Browne would never admit it smelled like dehydrated camel droppings—which it does if you're not smoking it. He performed a dramatic inhalation and said, "It's quite pleasant, actually, Franklin."

Before he got rolling I jumped in again, "I know smoking is a vice, Doctor, I really do. But I think most people have at least a couple of vices, don't you?"

"Well, I suppose that's true."

Off I ran again. "What vices do you have, Doctor? I'm sure they're only small ones." Then, sincere again: "I hope you don't think I'm nosey. I was just wondering."

I try to ask as many questions as I can, especially if he's being Friend or Father. He feels obliged to answer me so he can keep up the con, the pretence that we're having a nice chat. And that uses up part of the hour. Eventually he has to be "rude" and interrupt my inane questions to get us back on the path he intends us to walk that day. For another thing, asking questions helps me keep on top and better able to defend myself. He has to begin circling again, looking for another opening.

"Well, we are hardly here to talk about *me*, are we Franklin?" Browne liked rhetorical questions. He got back to the pipe. "No, I'm just interested in your pipe, there. It looks quite old. Briar, isn't it?"

"Ummm"—sincere look of concentration—"I'm not sure, Doctor. What's briar?"

"Briar is a dense wood. The boles on the roots are used in making pipes. I believe the best briar comes from the Mediterranean. The wood—"

He caught himself and steered back on course. "That pipe looks very well used. You must have got it from someone. A gift perhaps?"

See what I mean? How obvious could he get? The pipe *was* a gift, sort of, but one I certainly wasn't going to tell *him* about. It was the basis of his strategy this session. He saw it as a weak spot in the defences that I fought like hell to keep intact every day. He planned to get me talking about the pipe, where I got it and so on, until the wall was breached. Then he'd move past my defences and ransack my head for information. But you could see the attack coming miles away.

"Oh," I smiled, "I really can't remember *where* I got this pipe, Doctor. My memory isn't too reliable at times. I don't know why."

Browne had been sitting back in his large chair, his elbows resting on the arms. He was making a little steeple with his fingers. When I handed him the line about my memory he pounced forward and slapped his hands down onto the top of the desk.

"But you *do*, Franklin, you *do* know." He was as close as he ever came to a shout. "I've told you several times," he exclaimed impatiently, "we have blanks when our mind is hiding something it does not wish to confront and master. Memory blanks are *proof* that we need to talk these things out, Franklin. I've been through all this with you before."

"Well, yes. I guess I forgot."

He ignored that one, and sitting back, rebuilt the steeple. I don't know why he said "we" all the time. There was nothing wrong with *his* memory (or mine for that matter). Maybe he was trained in a kindergarten class.

"I sometimes wonder," he continued, "whether our memory lapses aren't a bit selective, Franklin."

"Doctor?" I was playing for time, now. My pipe had gone out so I slowly fished a match out of my shirt pocket and deliberately struck the match under the overhanging ledge of his desk. He pretended not to notice but you could almost hear him gritting his teeth, imagining the obscene streak of sulphur on the underside of his glowing, virginal desk top.

"What I mean," he explained with the patience of a school marm, "is that I think sometimes you are, um, putting me on. You forget significant things at significant times."

"What do you mean?" I asked, all innocence. "You merely inquired about my pipe and I said—"

"Look, Franklin, let's forget the pipe," he said, a little of the Firm approach slipping into his tone. "Let's just forget it. Our hour is passing quickly and I—"

"Yes, so it is," I interrupted, "and I certainly do enjoy—"

"Please don't interrupt," he shot back. Leaning forward again, arms on the desk, he linked his little sausages together into one tiny double fist. He meant business now.

"And please," he went on, "listen. I'm not pleased with your progress, Franklin. Not pleased at all. All along you've resisted my efforts to help you face your problems square on. But it must happen. It must. We ignore our inner problems at our peril. You were brought to this hospital extremely run down—physically—and on the verge of emotional disturbance. Nobody knows where you've been for the last few months. You refuse to tell us. You refuse to discuss *why* you ran away. You pretend—yes, pretend—don't give me that look—to forget what transpired during your absence. You will not even acknowledge the effects your actions have had on your poor parents. And, most dangerous of all, you avoid altogether the attempt to end your own life. You imagine, apparently, that no one can see that scar on your left wrist. Furthermore—"

"I think our time is up, Dr. Browne," I cut in. I leaned over and banged my pipe in the ashtray to get the ashes out. I'd had enough of this crap.

His pudgy face grew redder, like a round thermometer splashed with hot water.

"Don't interrupt me. And sit down in that chair."

Browne had never been like this before. His professional calm evaporated. He was becoming human before my eyes. But I'd had enough. My control was slipping too.

"I will not sit down. Don't order me around. Who the hell do you think you are, anyway? Do you think I'm a simpleton that you can manipulate day after day? *You* don't know *me!* You've never tried to *talk* to me like I was a human being. You think I'm just another nut case like those poor buggers you've got chained upstairs."

I was really rolling, now. A lot of junk was coming to the surface, demanding to be spit out.

"From the very beginning you've treated me like a two-year-old. I'm supposed to bare my bloody soul to a total stranger who's already decided I'm a suicide. Why don't we *talk* at these stupid meetings? Why—"

"I think you'd better stop now, Franklin," he said, his calmness returned. He wouldn't look me in the face. He pushed his glasses farther up his nose and said wearily, "You are a boy with some very serious prob—"

"And you," I fired back, "are an impertinent son of a bitch."

I stuck my pipe in my mouth and walked out, closing the door quietly behind me.

When I look back on my brief, empty relationship with Dr. Browne I sometimes wonder if, had he been a different kind of person, I'd have let my guard down.

Probably not, but you never know. There are some experiences you want to share with someone, as if the experience is somehow incomplete until you include the other person in its existence. But sometimes something happens that's so special, so much a part of what you are, you want to kind of *save* it, at least for a while. And maybe forever.

But if you save it in your head, the memories get newer memories piled on top of them, like old furniture in a dark attic, until you can't find the originals any more.

That's why I decided to write all this down in a journal. Just like in school. Only this time it's real.

Crabbe's Journal: 2

I've thought a lot about why I ran away from home and it's still pretty tough to put my reasons into a couple of tidy sentences. I've never been very good at explaining myself. Somehow, between the inside of my skull and the outside of my mouth the words get all changed around or they hide on me and I can't get hold of the ones I want. And I grew up in a house where I was *told* what I thought or how I should think. I wasn't asked. At school nobody is particularly interested in your feelings and they only pretend to be interested in your ideas.

Don't get me wrong. I'm not sorry I did what I did. Sure, sometimes I feel guilty about the fact that I scared my parents and relatives. But deep down I'm *glad* I did what I did. I'm glad because it's the one intelligent, independent, creative thing I've done in my life, and the one thing I've done for *me*.

I read a story one time, *The Loneliness of the Long Distance Runner*. It's about a teenager who grows up in some dirty, sooty slum in England. His father is dead, his mother is a runaround, his brother is a troublemaker. This guy is bitter about everything, especially his Dad's death and eventually gets into trouble and is sent to reform school. While he's there he hatches this plan that he thinks will get revenge on the "In-laws"—the people who obey the laws and have all the money. He's especially interested in getting back at the Warden of the reform school who finds out the kid can run fast and wants him to run for the school in the All England race and win the big trophy.

The kid knows the Warden is only using him, giving him extra privileges and things, so he can get the glory and show society how he's a wonderful rehabilitator of youth. So what does the kid do? He takes all the extras the Warden gives him. Then, on race day, he leads the pack for the whole race and, a dozen or so yards from the finish, in sight of the Warden and all the bigwigs and society types who pretend concern for kids like him, he stops. He just quits cold and stands staring defiantly at all of them. The other runners pass him and he loses.

See? Sometimes words don't count. They fly over people's heads or get trapped in the filters between their ears and their brains. Words are too easy to ignore, mis-understand, or twist around. Sometimes you have to *act* and sometimes so dramatically that people are stunned, stopped in their tracks. I don't say I escaped for only one reason, or that it was all revenge. I was sick of my life and already sick of the future that everybody had planned for me but nobody bothered to consult me about. I wanted to be free, to opt out of the plan. But, like the runner, I want-ed to do something that would symbolize what I thought and how I felt.

So I planned the escape carefully. It was to be the one perfect act I'd perform in my life: pure, clean, like the edge of a razor.

Crabbe's Journal: 3

To most people, running away without leaving a trace would be impossible. They leave breadcrumbs behind them; clues fall from them like scent. I was lucky. My father had taken me camping with him a few years earlier. It was the only trip we'd ever done together. I guess it was supposed to make up for all the years when he didn't know I existed. Anyway, I had overheard him telling a friend of his about the scenery but he'd forgotten the name of the lake and everything else about the trip. I was certain they'd never imagine their weak and unathletic son would ever run off to the woods.

I knew how to get to the lake and where we had put in that summer. There was a fishing lodge called Ithaca Camp on the shore of the lake—a bunch of cabins owned by a fat, friendly Greek with eight kids and a collie. You could launch a boat or canoe there for two bucks. But at the edge of the camp, a flat, calm river meandered into the lake. I knew that a sideroad crossed that river about half a mile upstream from Ithaca Camp. If I could hide the car in the bush near that bridge, get downriver past the camp and across the lake before dawn I would simply vanish. It would be like crossing the magic threshold in a myth.

Once I'd worked this out—over a period of a year or so—the rest was easy. So in the early spring of my final year I began to get serious about the preparations.

My father had stored all the camping stuff he'd bought for our glorious weekend in the wilds way back in a corner of the basement. I think he wanted to forget about his attempt to get two people who had trouble being in the same room together without some kind of spontaneous combustion breaking out to turn into pals over the course of one weekend. There were assorted packs, a little stove, a hatchet, knives, a pot set including dishes and cutlery, ropes—a whole store full of stuff. It was all piled behind and under old bundles of newspapers, magazines and boxes of forgotten junk. (My parents like to pretend this messy and dark part of their house doesn't exist.) When they were out one night, I went down and lugged what gear I wanted up to my room over the garage. Then I carefully replaced the junk and, just to be sure the place remained unvisited, I banged the light bulb to break the filament.

Once I had the stuff in my room I had to clean it and stow it out of sight of the maid. She isn't the hardest worker in the world so if I suggest there are areas of my room that don't need attention she willingly goes along with me. The little stove went up on the top shelf of my closet, rolled up in the sleeping bag. The pot set and hatchet went into a big steamer trunk that I keep all my unused sports equipment in. The trunk is hardly ever opened because I'm not very sporty: when my father used to have a flare-up of optimism and think maybe I *could* become a jock he'd buy me some expensive implement that was designed to hit, bash, or catch a ball, as if the mere presence of the object would add muscles to my frame and competitive spirit to what he often called my pansy mentality. I hung the packs in the closet behind my clothes. That done, I was ready for phase two.

I had to get hold of clothing and food in such a way that I left no clues. The clothing was easy. I picked out some old T-shirts, sweaters, socks, underwear and jeans, gave them to my mother and told her they were no good. She always gives our old clothes to the Salvation Army—after she has them cleaned by the help. I waited until they were ready and told her I'd drop them off at the collection bin which is in a shopping center parking lot on the way to school, but I kept them instead. So I managed to get two sets of clothes that no one would miss. They couldn't trace me if they didn't know what I was wearing.

The food was easier but took longer. I grabbed it from the kitchen when Cook, a grouchy old Polish lady who is as nearsighted as she is short-tempered, went home after work and my parents were out at one of their boring parties. I'd slip downstairs from my little eyrie and snaffle a few tins at a time. Just a few. The grumpy Polski is pretty sharp about her provisions. I added to this stockpile by buying what looked like useful and tasty stuff from local milk stores.

The food, as the spring wore on, gradually filled two of the big canvas canoe packs. That left a third for other gear and a small nylon haversack for clothing. By the end of May I was ready.

I figured I'd leave on a weeknight before my final exams, those big important keys that would, my parents deeply hoped, unlock dozens of university doors for me. In their fantasies I was to win piles of scholarships, much acclaim, and be the second *summa cum laude* of the Crabbe Clan (You Know Who was the first) and, eventually, I was to be famous. I'd be a rich corporate lawyer, a brilliant physician (specialist of course) or a big gun exec in a company that had wealth and power. I'd be My Parents' Son. That was the plan.

But I would not even write those phoney and moronic exams. I would slip quietly behind the curtain of the forest. I'd show them. By God, I'd show all of them.

Crabbe's Journal: 4

I don't know about you, but I sort of believe in omens. I'm not superstitious or anything like that; it's just that, sometimes, things fall into place for you (or on you). That's how I decided exactly which night to move out. Three "conversations" I had that day convinced me that the bridges behind me were pretty well burned.

First, my phys ed. teacher, Fat-Ass Grant, accidently discovered the Crabbe Family Secret. Which is kind of ironic because if ever there was a moronic excuse for a teacher Grant was it. He was king of jock city, the phys ed. department, and his idea of a stimulating lesson was to blow his whistle, roll a couple of basketballs out onto the court, and yell, "Okay, scrimmage! Warm up for ten minutes!" and waddle back into his office where he'd lower his two hundred into an old swivel chair and flip through a sports magazine for the rest of the period. Grant was lazy as well as fat. His T-shirttail never did make an acquaintance with the elastic waistband of his track pants, so there was always a band of greasy-looking flesh visible. His rear end was huge. That's what got him his nickname. There was a rumor that he was a frustrated basketball-player-reject who was on the booze regularly. I guess that qualified him for what he discovered about me.

I hated phys ed. and everything about it—the swamp smell of the locker room, the silly chirp of running shoes on the hardwood gym floor, the idiotic pointlessness of memorizing football rules or playing basketball with dozens of mini-Grants. So, usually, after Fat-Ass hit the swivel chair, I'd slip into the locker room, change, sneak out of the gym and grab a coffee across the street at Stephano's Grill. The Wednesday I'm talking about, I was sitting on the wooden bench putting on my socks when in walked Grant. He actually looked surprised when he saw me, as if he couldn't understand my passing up the joys of the court.

"What're you doing in here, Crabbe? You sick? The period isn't over yet. Why aren't you out on the floor? I said to scrimmage."

"Yea, didn't feel too well, Sir. Thought I'd get dressed 'n take it easy."

Grant's eyes became active. He stared at me. He thought he was on to something, like a fat, track-suited bug with his feelers doing overtime. I had stood up when he came in and, while I spoke to him, lifted one foot to get the second sock on. Mr. Cool. I should have stayed put. Because when I lifted my foot I lost my balance and sat down clumsily, half on, half off the bench. Then all off. My butt splotched into a small puddle of shower water. I laughed quietly, embarrassed.

"Oops! Sorry, Sir." What an idiot—apologizing for falling down. After all, it was my ass in the water.

He smiled the smile of a teacher who's got you dead to rights, and said with a sneer, "Crabbe, you look in bad shape." Then he walked over to me. His shoes squeaked on the floor.

"Stand up," he commanded.

I hauled myself to my feet, with a soggy rear end and one naked foot.

"Now get dressed. We're gonna have a talk."

I quickly got into the rest of my clothing, grabbed my books and athletic bag and followed him out of the locker room.

Halfway down the main hall he stopped and turned and said, "You've been drinking, haven't you, Crabbe?"

"What? Who, me? Drinking? No sir," I lied, not believing for a second I was going to talk my way out of *this* one. "What gave you that idea? Just because I slipped? The floor was wet."

"Crabbe, I know a slip from an alcoholic stumble. You didn't slip."

I gave up hope.

"Yeah, well I guess you *would* know the difference, Sir," I said sarcastically.

Grant's face got a little more tense.

"Don't get smart, Mister. Open that bag."

Before I could protest he yanked my bag out of my hand and began to rummage through it, finding nothing but seldom used gym clothes, worn out ballpoint pens and crumpled up paper.

He didn't give up.

"Okay, Crabbe. Let's check the locker."

"What do you mean?" I stammered.

"Your locker. Let's go check it. Where is it?"

He started down the hall again, barging along with a sense of mission. My locker was right outside the main office and we stopped in front of it.

I thought I'd try one last time.

"Really, Sir. My locker's my own prop—"

"Wrong, Crabbe," he interrupted. "The locker belongs to the school and it's on loan to you. Any teacher can demand access to it. Which is what I'm doing. Open up."

Hoping the fat creep's heart would give out before I finished the combination of the lock, I did as he demanded and opened the door. He took a quick look at the mess inside the locker, then he wrapped his beefy fist around the thermos bottle on the top shelf.

"What's this?" he said gleefully. "Didn't eat your soup today?" He shook it and heard the liquid sloshing around inside. Enjoying his triumph, he took a drink.

A lot of people would say I had a drinking problem. I'd have denied that. People only have a problem if they can't get what they want. My parents gave me a solid allowance and seldom asked me to account for it. I always had money for liquor. Buying it was easy. I'd drive to a suburb any time my supply ran low, and buy in quantity, mumbling some baloney about a party for my parents' anniversary. Then I'd use it up gradually, as needed. I used Silent Sam vodka, almost impossible to detect on my breath. I never got drunk. True, sometimes on a particularly bad day, begun by a tense breakfast with the riot squad, I'd begin to lose a bit of coordination (that's how Grant got me) by the end of the day, but that was rare. I didn't think I was a problem drinker. Far from it.

And I wasn't alone. My mother swallowed Valiums every day; my father drank heavily, if you counted the wonderful business lunches and what he poured down at home; lots of kids at school smoked grass regularly and drank at parties. I was no different.

So I was a little put out when Grant turned me in to the principal. He marched me right in, shoved me into a chair in the "salle d'attente" and went into the Beet's office as if he were a spy and had found the secret to end the war. I was a little scared, but not much because all this occurred *after* my plans had been laid. My only fear was that this would mess everything up or lead to expulsion from school. If I were expelled I couldn't make my point.

But I should have had more faith in the system (remember *The Loneliness of the Long Distance Runner?*). When I was ushered into the Beet's office—we called him that because he was short, stocky, florid in complexion, big eared and completely bald—he was sitting there with my student record open in front of him.

"Sit down, Crabbe," he said, man-to-man. "I see you're in a bit of trouble."

Frazer tried to be very English most of the time, so he thought understatement was clever. He made me retell the story of my being caught by Fat-Ass, then gave me a little lecture about relying on a drug "like a crutch." How could a man with a bulbous nose on which the veins look like bright red highways and whose hands were stained with nicotine be such a hypocrite? Did dopes like Grant and Frazer think they were kidding anybody?

He ended up by letting me off. No punishment. Why? Because I was an honor student, scholarship material, graduating whiz kid. And, although he didn't mention it, because my old man was Rich and Influential and they both belonged to the same golf club. If I'd gone into that office with dirty jeans, messed-up hair and faceless parents he'd have crucified me. But the system protects its own.

I left, smiling inside, but contemptuous of the whole stupid arrangement. But the smile soon faded. He might phone home.

Dinner was, to use the Beet's understatement, a little tense. I knew my parents had got the call because my mother was unusually precise in her table manners and overly polite to me. "Be kind enough to pass the chops to your father, dear"—that sort of thing. Nothing could penetrate her good breeding, or the Valium and dinner wine.

My father was Dressed for Dinner as usual. He was very exact in his opinions about manners and appearances. Good breeding again. The brass candelabra was in place— a quirk of my parents. It stood in the center of our dining room table on a hand-crocheted, ivory-colored doily—a great, ponderous imitation Something-or-Other that clutched three white candles. It wasn't even impressive. It was just silly.

So picture this: There was Father Crabbe, wealthy corporate lawyer, dressed formally in a dark suit at one end of our six-foot oak table; there was the thin Worried Mother placed at the center of one side, dressed in a burgundy pant suit with a hint of jewelry and her hair dyed a kind of blondish color; and opposite Dad was My Son the Problem, dressed in a black T-shirt and jeans, a little smashed (for this pow-wow I needed help), trying to read Father's mood through the groping brass arms of that stupid contraption, waiting for the other shoe to drop.

All the ingredients for a third-rate soap opera.

Once dessert was served, we were all ready to begin the scene that we knew had been written for us by eighteen years of life together. I don't want to record everything that was said. It isn't necessary. My mother got hysterical, wept, clutched her napkin in her hands, criticized my ingratitude and laid out the inventory of how lucky I was and all they'd done for me. My father took the other line, lecturing me in what he thought was a reasonable voice about how I should use my God-Given Talents to make something of myself—which meant getting money in large quantities—and stay away from leftwingers, eggheads, and so on and on and on. I, as usual, attacked their entire way of life, their snobbery and materialism, saying I couldn't be grateful for a way of life I found meaningless and contemptible—and other cruel and pointless things.

All this began with a question from my father: "I thought I told you if you were ever caught drinking again…" and I swear he had his third brandy in his hand when he said it.

If only we could have broken the pattern we'd lived in so long. If only someone had written a new score. But there we were, playing the same piece, out of tune, out of sync, the only one we ever played, the only one we knew.

At the end we left the table. They went their way, I went mine. Their way was another party.

Those three conversations—with Grant, Frazer and my parents—were the omens that told me tonight was the night to go. I was as ready as I'd ever be, I thought. So I began to prepare for my escape, a little depressed, a little scared, and a little under the care of Silent Sam.

Digression

One thing I learned pretty quickly at high school was that it doesn't pay to be honest, to be yourself. I had already learned to play the game at public school but at high school they stuck it to me really good. The thing was, they'd ask you questions but they didn't listen to you; they weren't interested in what you said. Why ask a question if you don't care what the answer is? What the teachers really wanted you to do was guess what they *wanted* you to answer and if you guessed correctly (not that it was hard) you were "right."

But it took me a little while to learn that. For instance, our grade nine History teacher, Miss Wase, once said to us, "Now, class, I want you people to use your brains today to solve a big problem. Imagine you are all shipwrecked on an island with no adults around. It is a tropical island outside the shipping lanes so it doesn't look like you'll be rescued for a long time, if at all. You must organize yourselves in some way. How would you begin?"

We all sat around a minute looking mystified. Nobody put up their hands. But I remembered this interesting book

I had read a year or so before called *Lord of the Flies* and I thought I had a pretty good idea. I put up my hand.

"Yes, Franklin?"

Stupid me, thinking she was really interested in my opinion. I started telling her about the novel and said that since there were no adults around we kiddies would have to form a government and democracy wouldn't work because we were immature and uneducated and blah, blah, blah, and I ended up suggesting a dictatorship that would be temporary and then she interrupted.

"Thank you, Franklin; that will do for a start. Now, class, let's go back for a moment."

Surprised that she interrupted me, I sat down, beaming and smiling hoping that my answer was really good and thinking this was one teacher who might like me. Then I looked at her face. It was clouded with anger, although she tried to hide it. My smile disappeared and a fast hot wave rolled through me. I felt wounded and embarrassed. I had ruined her lesson by jumping ahead and running through the ideas she had wanted us to struggle with all period as she led us from point to point. We were supposed to end up where *she* wanted us to—ready to begin a study of government in Ancient Greece.

I realized all this in a split second of agonizing humiliation. And when I was leaving at the end of the period she said, "You know, Franklin, it isn't necessary to try to impress *me* by telling everything you know."

The same kind of thing happened in French a couple of days later. Our teacher would ask for volunteers to go up to the board and I'd stick up my mitt every time. After a couple of times, he didn't ask me any more. Because what he was doing was he'd get kids to put up answers he hoped would be incorrect so he could use them to teach us really earthshaking stuff like not getting "le" and "la" mixed up, all the while making sarcastic remarks. So it didn't pay to be right there either.

After that I started to check out all my teachers and I realized they all wanted the class to go along with their plans for the lessons—that is, those who *had* a plan—some of them, like "Beaker Baker" the chem guy, just hemmed and hawed and rambled all period. They all asked a lot of questions but, like I said, none of them were really interested in what you said. And the last thing they wanted was for you to think.

But if you do think about it, school is stupid and ass-backward anyway. The people who know the answers ask the questions. And the people who don't know the answers answer the questions!

So anyway, we all made an unspoken truce. I minded my business and wrote their stupid tests and did their equally stupid assignments (most of them) and got by with dandy marks. During class I'd watch some movie behind my eyes or read, using the old book-inside-the-text trick. I played their game and won all kinds of points and prizes and crap that I secretly hated. But nobody asked me what I thought of them.

That went on for a few years until I got Peters for grade twelve English. He woke me up again.

He walked into class the first day, all packed full of importance and plans—obviously a new teacher—and said, "Now, let's get something straight, class. You are here to learn to *think,* not to memorize Shakespeare or draw plot graphs or expect me to give you all the answers. If you are an intellectual slob or mentally sloppy I'll come down on you like a big truck. But if you try to think your way along and take an active part in class discussions I'll see that you get an English credit. Now, let's get started."

Of course, everybody figured this was baloney and a few of the guys tried to make it hard for the new teacher but Peters ended their nonsense pretty quickly. After a couple of weeks went by the kids were still shell-shocked, wondering why this guy did everything differently.

One day he said, "Crabbe, stick around after class is over." I did. While the next class was filing into the room he said with that machine-gun delivery of his, "Look, Crabbe I'm disappointed in you. I've read your essay and I've read your file at the Guidance office. You write like a poet and your I.Q. is higher than mine, which is 150—not that I believe much in I.Q.s. I want you to get off your butt and do some contributing in this class. You should be one of the leaders and you just sit there reading everything but what you're supposed to. I want a change. Starting tomorrow. Understand?"

"Yes Sir," I said.

"Good. Now get to class or you'll be late." Then he smiled.

Peters was like that. He talked like a tough guy but he read poems like you were sure he was going to cry. And he always managed to slip a compliment into his talk to you. You didn't notice it until later, then it made you feel good. If a kid made a mistake in class, Peters always managed to make the kid feel good about the goof. He'd say something like, "If you knew all the answers, you wouldn't need me or this school, would you?"

I'll bet they hated him in the staff room. He always needed a haircut; he wore the goofiest looking baggy clothes you've ever seen draped over his five-foot two-inch frame. His tie was dirty and wrinkled and he wore a cardigan rather than a sports coat or suit jacket. And he had three or four pairs of fancy, pointy-toed cowboy boots. He was always dropping books on his rapid, commotion-filled transit down the halls. I swear, he actually *slid* around corners.

I'll bet they hated him in the staff room because every time he went in there, stepping over all the old bones and dead wood, he'd remind them just by being there that they were all dead and what they were doing was a hoax, draining all the creativity out of us. Peters was like one of those machines we played with in physics where you'd wind a handle and wheels would turn and then a spark would jump between two metal balls. He was always charged up and his energy jumped into his students.

My father thought Peters was a dangerous man who would undermine the school and in a way he was right— but for the wrong reasons: my father's criticism was based on the clothing. Peters *did* threaten the system. He made us think. But nobody wants a thinker. Thinkers are irritating and troublesome and they don't fit in. Our school wanted everything to be smooth and I had been going along with them all for years. Peters made me break the truce. I began to ask myself again and again about my future and eventually I decided to cut out of the herd. The thing with teaching people to think is that you never know *where* they'll end up.

Crabbe's Journal: 5

My parents left for the club at about eight. Since they seldom returned before one or two I figured I had lots of time. As they left I was enjoying the last bath I'd have in a long time. When Cook slammed the back door I was packing my toothbrush.

As soon as it was dark, I began.

From my room above the garage a wooden staircase descends to the back patio, and behind the stairs is a door into the garage. It's kind of hard to get at because the stairs were put in after the garage was built. They were a fire escape from my room. The city made my parents put it in when they had the room over the garage built so I could have my own turf.

I began to move the gear from the hiding places, haul it downstairs in the dark, into the garage and into the back of our station wagon. Within an hour I had all the stuff transferred. It was almost ten o'clock when I started on the canoe. This was tricky. The boat was kept on two saw-horses behind the garden shed at the foot of the yard, between the shed and a high cedar hedge. The whole plan rested on my being able to get out of the neighborhood without anyone seeing that canoe. So I had to work in the dark.

First, I turned out the lights of all the rooms along the back of the house. The yard was now good and dark. Then I went to the tool shed, slipped behind, and tried to lift the canoe from the horses. Graceful creature that I am, I lost my balance and fell, knocking over the saw-horses and ended up pinned between the shed and the canoe. I was sure the clatter and banging woke the world. I lay there for five minutes, breathing quietly, straining for sounds of alarm or roving neighbors, or suspicious detectives in creased raincoats carrying big, shiny flashlights. Nothing stirred.

Dragging myself out of the trap, I grabbed one edge of the canoe and dragged it from the space between the shed and the hedge. Once clear of the saw-horses and pieces of old lumber, it slipped easily on its bottom over the damp grass. I put it down and went back quickly to right the saw-horses and haul the tarp over them. As an afterthought I took some butt-ends of lumber and propped them up under the tarp. It looked as if the canoe was still there. Pleased with this ruse I picked up one end of the boat again and half-lifted, half-dragged it across the sixty or so feet of grass to the patio. I had to hoist it completely off the ground then so it wouldn't scrape on the flagstones.

I confess I am not good at lifting things. I am skinny, gangly, and not strong. But I don't think even Hercules could get sixteen feet of fiberglass canoe behind a staircase and through a door into a garage. I couldn't do it. I pulled, pushed, swore, lifted, yanked, begged. No dice. My only other choice was to lug the thing around to the front of the house through the big garage doors, but that was too risky. So I tried again. I hauled the front of the canoe to the top of the doorway and jammed it into the top of the door-jamb. The rear point was wedged into the angle where the stairs hit the patio. Great. Not only did the thing look ridiculous, I couldn't move it at all, now. Cursing, I kicked the damn thing. It broke free of its perch, bow first, and thundered to the ground, half in the door, half out, knocking over a garbage pail and setting up a pounding clamor. I quickly went into the garage (not easy because I had to climb over the boat) and dragged the boat in. I closed the door and held my breath.

Fifteen minutes later I had the roof racks attached to the wagon. Getting the canoe on top was a strain. I found that swearing helped a whole bunch. By the time I had it tied down securely, with big, lumpy knots I guessed would hold, it was almost midnight. At the last minute I remembered that paddles might come in handy.

I was almost ready to go. I had just climbed into the station wagon to check the route to Ithaca Camp on the roadmap for the thousandth time and was straining to see by the interior light when I heard a sound that chilled my blood.

A car had pulled into the driveway. My parents had come home early.

Quickly slamming the wagon door, I rolled onto the floor—just in time, because the electric door on the other side of the garage began to grind open, allowing the yellowy-white light from the headlights to splash into the darkness of the garage and throw eerie shadows up the walls and across the ceiling. I lay looking up at the roof of the wagon, as if the harder I stared the safer I was. My heart's pounding roared in my ears. If they so much as glanced at the wagon, with that big red canoe on top, I was sunk.

The long, black, rocket-like car my father drives growled into the garage. The engine quit. The light disappeared. The garage door clanked shut. There was a moment of dead quiet, then doors opened and shut, echoing. Feet scraped and clicked on the cement floor. The sounds were distant, hollow.

So were the tired voices.

"I don't want to talk about it any more. The kid's going to have to work this all out for himself. I'm sick of the whole issue. It goes on and on. Do you want the light on?"

"No, I can find my way. That's easy for you to say. Very easy. But you don't have to watch him flush his life down the drain. Because that's what he'll do if we let him. He's not going to university. You know that, don't you?"

"What do you mean I don't have to watch him? I'm his father, for Christ's sake...."

The door to the house opened, then closed again, muffling their voices.

My heartbeats continued to leap all over the inside of my body for a few minutes. I was sweating through my shirt and surprised to find I was breathing quickly. But I was safe. I sat up in the front seat of the car. I would be behind schedule because I couldn't leave for a couple of hours, now. That would mean—I did some quick calculations—I'd arrive near Ithaca Camp just about dawn, early enough to be under the cover of darkness but too late to set out across the lake. So I'd have to hide in the bush near the river for twenty-four hours. I sat back in the seat and waited.

I felt good on the long journey North, sort of free. It didn't take long to get out of the city and away from the lights and pretty soon I was sifting along in the darkness, in a moving cave, cowboy music on the radio and the wind singing in the ropes that held the canoe on.

Well, I was almost happy.

Crabbe's Journal: 6

I drove off the main highway about an hour before dawn, and turned down the secondary highway, traveling about thirty miles until I reached a small town whose name I've forgotten. Noelville, or something like that. The main street of the town hit the highway at right angles and I turned right, quickly leaving behind a row of wood frame stores, a bank, a hotel and a straggle of wooden bungalows. In the near dawn the buildings looked tired and defeated.

About twenty miles outside of town, well into the bush, signs advertising Ithaca Camp began to appear. The road was narrower here and the blacktop had turned to gravel a long time ago. I had to watch carefully for the logging road I wanted but managed to find it and turned the station wagon onto it just as the sky was beginning to brighten. I had met no other cars since I had left the main highway.

The logging road hadn't been used since the previous autumn by the look of the heavy layer of leaves—a good sign. I had to drive slowly. Branches that canopied the track whacked the side of the wagon and thumped hollowly against the canoe. I drove for about ten minutes until I spotted a good hiding place for the car—a big stand of evergreens packed fairly close together but allowing room to ram the wagon into the middle of them. I could barely get the door open.

Stretching my creaky limbs (I hadn't dared to stop except to take a leak, so had driven all night) I looked around and caught sight of the river through the branches. It was a dull, gray color in the flat lighting. The forest was quiet; only light birdsong could be heard. The air was chilly.

Always listening for motors or voices, I spent a few hours doing hard work. First, I unloaded the packs and dragged them down to the river bank, covering them with leaves in case a fishing boat happened along. Then I hauled the canoe down from the roof of the wagon, banging it and my head against the branches above the station wagon, and dragged it near the packs where I covered it with branches and leaves. Last, I cut boughs to hide the car even better than it was already.

Satisfied that the family auto would escape the notice of anyone who wasn't looking for it, I sat down in a sunny patch near the river but out of sight, leaned back against a tree and munched on a chocolate bar. I'll tell you, some chocolate bars taste better than others. That one was the best I've ever had.

The afternoon sun was warm and I was tired. A fresh breeze fooled around with the branches, rustling the dead leaves that clung to the trees since the previous autumn. The big river looked flat, lazy and slow, murmuring gently as it slipped by. I fell asleep.

I awoke once in the dark a little chilly and dug my sleeping bag out of the pack. In a wink I was bundled up and back asleep. The next time I opened my eyes it was about an hour before dawn—the time I always get up at home. I have to. I can never get to sleep again. But this morning something was missing: the churning in my stomach that told me my nerves were getting ready for another day.

After taking a drink from the river I set quickly to work. The sky was clear and starry with plenty of light.

Lifting the canoe to the water and launching it was lesson number one. On the first try I half-dragged, half-lifted it to the water—but not too well because it went in cockeyed and took on a couple of gallons of river. So I dragged it out again, rolled it over to dump out the water, and tried again a few yards downriver where the bank sloped more gradually into the water. Fine. I went back for the gear and turned around just in time to see the canoe floating gently downstream. It cost me two legs wet to the crotch to retrieve it. That was when I thought it would be a good idea to attach a rope to the bow.

That done, I tied the boat to a log on the bank and went back for the packs. Manhandling a huge pack filled with mostly tinned food into a canoe that bobs and tips with every move you make is no easy task, especially when you have to do it twice. And a third time, for the equipment pack. It was no consolation that I'd be eating my way through the food.

But, I did it. I got it all in, stowed the extra paddle—then looked anxiously for a place to sit. I'd only been in a canoe with another person (You Know Who). Did I sit in the teeny seat at one end that was situated almost at the point? Or in the slightly wider one at the other end, which at least had some leg room? I tried the first. I had no leg room because of the packs and when I sat down the other end of the boat shot out of the water and remained suspended in mid-air. And my ass was about one inch from the water.

This can't be it, I thought.

I got out and stared at the arrangement for a minute. Then a thought struck me. I (regretfully) dragged the three heavy packs, which I had stowed wherever they fit, and placed two of them, resting on the long edges, side by side behind the narrower of the two seats. I threw the haversack that held my clothes into the little space in front of that seat (almost bouncing it into the river). Then I took the third big pack and put it in the center of the boat, just behind the thwart.

Carefully, I got in again and gingerly sat down. The craft seemed to sit flat on the water. I was very pleased with myself.

Until I remembered I had brought no lifejacket. Oh, well, too late now.

Time was passing. I wanted to be past Ithaca Camp and way out onto the lake by light, so I pushed off into the current.

I don't know nearly enough funny words to describe the way my brave craft and I traveled down that river. If I'd had to paddle upstream rather than down I'd *still* be there, cursing and weaving and turning complete circles in the middle of the river and bumping the banks. I realized in about five seconds that paddling a canoe by yourself (in the dark too!) was a lot harder than sitting in the front putting the blade into the water every once in a while as the person in the back does all the work. I guess I imagined the thing steered itself.

As soon as I accomplished one stroke, the current took the canoe over and I was more or less part of the baggage. Near the lake as it was, the river was wide, flat and slow, and I could *almost* guide the boat along. I went backwards part of the time, turned a couple of three-sixties, and nudged a few logs and rocks, but I made it, safe and a bit scared, to the river mouth.

It was daybreak by then. There was a gray-white smear on the horizon that showed a sky beginning to cloud over. At the river mouth I ran into a sandbar just beneath the surface and had to step out into the ice cold water and drag the canoe over the bar and into the lake.

Luckily, there was just a faint breeze. My humorous and inefficient paddling made it slow going. I'd get in a couple of strokes on the right, sending me in a foward arc toward the left shore. Changing sides and repeating the motion pushed me to the right. Thus, I zigged and zagged toward a large stand of white trees on the farther shore that, I remembered, marked the way out of the lake. As I was anxious to get across the water, which was about two miles wide, I paddled hard and was soon tired. After I'd worked for an hour and was halfway across I turned to look back at the camp. With relief I saw that I was certainly too far away to be describable.

After what seemed like ages, I made the far shore, letting the canoe scrape softly onto a beach. All my muscles were sore and complaining, especially arms and shoulders, and I was breathing hard. Blisters had begun to form across my palms and in the hollows of my thumbs. All this after only two miles! Still, I felt a sense of accomplishment. Out of sight of the camp, I was officially free.

Strange how that word soon took on new and unexpected meaning.

Crabbe's Journal: 7

If the river *into* the lake was kind to me, moving me carefully from where I left the station wagon to the lintel of the sandbar, the stream *out* of the lake was playful. For one thing, it was narrow, about the width of a canoe. For another, it moved quickly. It twisted and snarled and backtracked all through a sort of pass between a group of hills. One minute the stream was so shallow that I couldn't paddle, even if I *did* know how; then the sandy bottom would disappear suddenly into a deep dark pool, usually on a bend. Occasionally there were log jams or boulders to avoid. The shore was sometimes crowded with bushes; sometimes grassy and swampy for about fifty yards to the trees; sometimes a graveyard of bleached stumps.

But I didn't have time to notice how creepy it all was. Through this scenery I tried, with almost continual failure, to control the canoe. I hated those long curves and sharp, double-back bends the most because the current would always move me into the bend and push me into the bank. Then I'd have to struggle and heave and splash my way out of the backwater and into the straightaway below the curve.

After what was easily a couple of hours of this bone-grinding toil I began to get a little bit of control. It was during one of the many rest stops, canoe jammed against a grassy bank by the current, that I decided I might as well experiment with my paddle to try and gain at least some control. I had nothing to lose, that's for sure. So, I'd paddle easily in the straight sections, changing sides quickly, then when one of those frustrating curves came I'd drag the paddle and try to steer. I found that by turning the paddle different ways I could sort of rudder the canoe in roughly the direction I wanted. And by "ruddering" on different sides, I got even more satisfaction. It didn't work *all* that well: I still got trapped in backwaters and shoved around in the bends and I still thumped logs and ground on gravel bars—once I even dropped my paddle over the side while changing hands, barely managing to retrieve it—but things improved.

The river began to widen, straighten and slow down now and the shoreline was not so hilly. Luckily: I needed the rest and paddling was easier. Soon I was slipping, in a zig-zag of course, across a huge beaver pond. The surface of the coffee-colored water was sprinkled with tired-out looking lily pads. But I was far more weary than the plants. As long as I kept moving, my body stayed numb, but when I rested, the aches and pains started, and my muscles, apparently every one on my body, began to stiffen. Well, there'd be no rest for a while.

At the far end of the pond was a beaver dam that spanned a natural rock cut about a dozen feet across. From the dam the water dropped roaring about six feet over boulders and fallen tree trunks. If I remembered right, from the trip with my father, the creek rushed and jumped through the bush for a quarter of a mile, over many tiny falls. To get from beaver pond to lake you walked along a portage that followed the creek.

I was glad to get out of that canoe, I'll tell you. My legs would hardly straighten but I managed to stand up, clamber over the packs and step out onto the little sand beach. It seemed like I hadn't felt land under my boots for a long time. I swivelled my torso a little and flapped my arms, then walked into the bush to take a leak. I returned to find the canoe being dragged from the beach toward the falls. I'd have to watch that.

I admit I'd never done a day's work in my life before I escaped. Our house had electric this and power that. What work the machines didn't do alone, they helped with. And the servants did the rest. Clothes always arrived clean, food always arrived cooked, lawns were always mowed. We never walked where we could drive (and if we couldn't drive we wouldn't go). We even hired someone else to fix the machines if they got sick or died.

So that portage, after many hours of paddling, was an ordeal completely beyond my experience. When my father and I did it, we had much less baggage and a portage wagon—a sheet of plywood with a bicycle wheel underneath—to help. All we had to do was pull the thing.

I dragged the packs out of the boat and put them to the side. Then I hauled the canoe up onto dry land. I'd seen pictures of guys carrying canoes, jaunting along happily through a natural wonderland, heads invisible under the noble craft that rested lightly on their shoulders. Sure. You bet. Just try to get the damn thing up. I attempted everything, from every direction, but the canoe just rolled out of my hands and fell to the ground with a hollow thump. Luckily, it was fiberglass. Then, in desperation, I rolled it onto one gunwale, crawled in under it, settled the center thwart on my shoulders, and staggered to my feet. Success! I had it off the ground—until the front end slowly descended and thumped the ground, sending hollow echoes drumming into my ears. I slid my arms farther forward on the gunwales and heaved, sending the bow skyward at great speed and ramming the stern into the dirt behind me. More echoes. Easy, now, I thought. I adjusted the position of my hands again, pulled down on the gunwales and slowly raised the back and then, gingerly, because the balance wasn't good, I began to walk.

A quarter of a mile isn't far—once around a track, a few city blocks—but when you're trying to balance a clumsy chunk of fiberglass and wood, whose weight is concentrated into a three-inch wide thwart across your already aching shoulders, while bumping over rocks and slipping in mud, a quarter mile is a journey. Not only that, it's a boring journey because with the boat overhead all you can see is a yard of ground in front of your toes.

After a couple of forevers I caught sight of water through the bare trees and finally reached the lake. So as not to drop the boat I knelt down on the gravelly shore and tried to ease out from under. I ended up sort of rolling it off my shoulders as I fell sideways. I lay there for a while, panting, then sat up.

The walk back through the open bush, mostly tall hardwoods, seemed heavenly in comparison. I could hear the brook racing over the mossy stones, birds telling their chirpy stories, my boots thumping on the dry ground or slicking through mud in the low spots.

But it didn't last. Carrying the packs was worse than the canoe. Each of the big ones was heavier than the boat and I'd packed them like a fool. They were shapeless blobs, like ripe grapes or water bags, except the food tins or equipment stuck sharp corners out. I probably looked pretty funny trying to get them on my back (one at a time, of course). I couldn't *lift* them on so I tried a few experiments and ended up dragging a pack to a flat spot on the embankment and sort of half-sitting, half-leaning against it from below, slipping my arms in under the straps. I stood up and staggered off down the trail.

Within two minutes I had decided to repack those bags first chance I got. Because, aside from the leather straps cutting into the already tender muscles of my shoulder, cutting off the blood so that my arms began to buzz, all kinds of corners and ends of objects—mostly *hard* objects—dug into my back, like cruel fingers prodding me along. I put out more sweat on that portage in one go-round than I had in all my life up till then. After four trips I was soaked. At the end of the last trip I sat down dizzily and looked out over the lake.

A breeze had come up during the hour and a half I was on the trail and the lake had a bit of a chop to it. The cloud cover was lower and the whole scene was gray and colorless. It was getting late but I knew the campsite I was heading for was only a mile or so down the lake. My father and I had stayed there.

Did I say a little farther? Well, maybe, in a boat paddled by a skillful canoeist. But for old Crabbe, landlubber from birth, another challenge because I had the waves to contend with. I'm not saying they were huge rollers. They were barely ripples—just enough to make the canoe roll a little off center as each one passed under me. I was traveling at right angles to wind and waves. And the breeze—just enough to flip my forelock every few minutes—was no help. The Crabbe zig-zag *almost* worked on flat, calm water with dead still air. Here I traveled in four directions at once: the zig, the zag, the gradual forward motion toward the campsite and the sideways drift caused by wind and wave (breeze and ripple). It took another hour and a half.

But I did it. I got to the place, a narrow, rocky peninsula about fifty feet across the base and twice as long covered with pines. I groaned with relief when I heard the bow grind into the rock of the shore. Climbing stiffly out of the canoe, I stood up and stretched as much as my muscles would let me. Then I dragged the canoe up on shore, manhandled the packs out and hauled them up the slanting rock onto flat, needle-covered ground.

I was worn out, beaten thin. And what I wanted was sleep. Soon I had the tent pitched (a little cock-eyed but standing under a huge pine. And a few seconds after that I crawled gratefully into my sleeping bag and took a long, graceful dive into the black well of sleep.

If I'd known what was going to happen I wouldn't have made that dive.

Crabbe's Journal: 8

I returned to the world slowly, keeping my eyes closed though wakefulness was almost complete. I could smell the damp, still, pine-scented air, then the unique smell of wet nylon. The sounds of falling water surrounded me: big, well-spaced plops from the tall pine that stretched above the tent and delicate drips onto the tent fly.

I opened my eyes. The inside of the tent was filled with a warm, thin, rosy light as daylight was filtered by the orange walls of the tent. I lifted the flap to find a gray, rainy day outside. The lake was tea-colored and calm.

I was warm and cozy inside the down sleeping bag. But as wakefulness came it brought a variety of aches and pains. My body had a work hangover that would win prizes. And the edges of rocks and roots under the nylon floor of the tent didn't help. I snuggled deeper and dozed again.

But I couldn't sleep. After a while I got out of the cocoon and crawled into the day. I tied back the tent flaps and looked around. Gray. Close. Wet. It was the kind of day you'd like to spend in bed with an interesting novel and a bit of Silent Sam to help you keep away the Meanies. I had brought no booze but the rest of the plan sounded good.

First I ambled back into the bush a little ways, muscles complaining the whole way. The soggy, needle covered ground was dead quiet. While I was taking a leak I looked around and saw some strange animal droppings, almost like cow-flaps, all over the place. But there were no cows around here. I took no further notice and went back to the campsite.

Foresight has never been a strong point with me, as I was reminded when I started to rummage around in the packs. I had left the one holding the equipment wide open last night and now it was soaked inside and out. One of the food packs had come partially open with all the handling from the day before and the rain had invaded it too. The few thick novels I'd packed were sopping wet all through. The pages separated when I tried to turn them. No booze and now no books. This trip was going to be a challenge.

My snacks were wet too. Since swimming peanuts have never been my favorite food, I scattered a half pound of them around for the squirrels and dug out a tin of smoked herring and a bag of "chocolate dreams." Then I retied the packs, took a long drink from the lake and hauled my aching frame back into the tent.

With my boots off and stashed in a front corner of the tent, I climbed back into the bag and managed to pack it around me in such a way that I could sit cross-legged with my arms free. I peeled back the lid of the kipper can and gorged on the oily fish, stuffing the morsels into my mouth with my fingers. Boy, what a classy guy. But I was famished. I managed in my talented way to spill fish oil on my sleeping bag, the tent floor, and the ground in front of the tent. Otherwise, I was very neat. The chocolates tasted dreamy, as advertised on the label. I munched through half the bag and stuffed the rest into one of my boots.

Then I did something I've never done. I just sat and looked out through the rain across the campsite, past the well-spaced pines and over the lake. My mind was unusually calm. Little wavelets of thought rippled across it, leaving no trace. It was—nice; it was nice to sit and look away at nothing in particular. Because ordinarily my mind felt like a telephone exchange, constantly jabbed and zapped by frantic messages: test coming Monday, Mother mad again, project due two days ago, kids laughing behind me in the halls. On and on, over and over, current never turned off, switchboard never shut down, messages unanswered, circuits overloaded.

But here I noticed the millions of tiny currents that streaked the surface of the dark water. The far shore was a soft, dark gray line. Shreds of cloud changed shape quickly, moving across the somber sky. Water, land and sky were blended together, unified by the hiss of the rain.

Imagine. I thought all these thoughts as I sat like a skinny, aching buddha in my little orange cave. Tough Crabbe, who hated city rain because all it did was move the grime from one place to another. Resting in that orange tent I looked out into a very small world, shut off by rain and distance. I was contented. I was even almost happy. I was also tired, so I rolled over and fell asleep.

I woke up with a start from a dream troubled by dark wings, one of those nightmares that leaves you with no memory, only fear. The tent flaps were still open and through them lay a black night, like a wall. It was dead silent—no wind, no dripping of rain. The air was chilly and damp.

Rolling onto my back, I pulled the bag up around my neck and stared at the tent roof. I couldn't shake the feeling of foreboding that enclosed me as if it were part of the night air. Had I had a nightmare, brought on by the food I ate just before sleep? I remembered nothing.

Anxiety attacks were not new to me; they had introduced me to Silent Sam and visited me regularly. But this was different. This was a dark, nameless fear that I seemed to breathe in with each breath. And I could hear nothing and see nothing. My senses were useless.

Then a strange sound separated itself from the night—a soft, tearing sound off in the woods behind me, like the ripping of wet paper. Then, nothing, only my breathing. My heartbeat picked up. I strained to hear and to see. Another sound. Different, closer, a brushing noise. Then, as one slowly becomes aware of a rising breeze, I felt an eerie huffing sound, almost like the snort of a pig, but not as sharp, or the pant of a dog, but more threatening. It was rhythmical. It got slowly louder. A twig snapped back of the tent. One of the guy lines jerked. By now my pulse was hammering in my ears but I could still follow the movement of the huffing noise from behind the tent along the side, coming closer and louder. I jerked up onto one elbow as a searing terror burned through me.

A shape blacker than the night loomed in the doorway. The huffing was loud now as the shape pumped stinking breath into the tent. I was paralyzed, convinced that some shaggy monster had shambled from a horrible fairy tale to tear my flesh and break my bones.

The shape stopped moving. "Oh God, oh God," I chanted, my eyes fixed on the shape. The air inside the tent reeked from the foul odor. Unable to keep still any longer, I shrieked and tried to scramble to the back wall of the tent. The shape leapt at me, snarling. I felt sharp claws through the sleeping bag dragging me backwards. Instinctively I rolled into a ball, whimpering, "No, no, no," and kept still. The claws withdrew.

Another snarl filled the tent as I was seized again and partially rolled over. Eyes squeezed shut, jaws clamped closed as in a seizure, I stopped breathing, petrified.

I must have fainted—for how long I don't know. But when I came to again it was light, the flat light of an overcast dawn. I was lying half-in, half-out of the tent, my head resting on my arm. The stench around me was awful, almost physical. I then realized I had thrown up. My head and arm were lying in sticky vomit. I got up on one elbow and threw up again in painful spasms, until nothing more came. My stomach continued to heave and I lay back down, head on arm. A few minutes later, still panting from terror and the heaving, I struggled to a sitting position at the door of the tent. I saw the sleeping bag twisted and rolled into a corner. Down covered everything like gray snow. One of my boots was missing. The other had been chewed around the top. The candy bag was ripped and empty.

Turning my head I looked over the campsite. Nothing there—except a brown, smelly pile of the same animal droppings I'd seen in the bush. Then I noticed that the food packs had been dragged around a little, but neither had been torn open.

When I got to my hands and knees I realized with disgust that sometime during my ordeal my bowels had emptied a liquid, stinking mess into my pants and down both legs. I had pissed myself too. The disgusting stench of myself nauseated me further and I began to retch again as I crawled toward the lake.

Slowly, looking fearfully around, for I half expected to be attacked again, I removed my clothing. I searched for claw marks but found nothing. At last I sat naked at the edge of a lake, like a newborn baby—weak, scared and dirty. After a few minutes I stood and shakily waded into the cold, numbing water. I washed myself clean of my own filth, sweat and fear.

The clouds began to lift and allow the sun to bring a little warmth. After I washed, I lay on the flat granite shingle. Slowly the sun warmed the fear out of me. Relief replaced it. I was still alive.

I had been certain I was going to die, torn and chewed by a black bear (I guessed that's what it had to be), my remains left to rot alone in the bush. Somehow, I'm not sure why, dying like that scared me more than a glorious death on a battlefield or in a bicycle race or something like that. It sounds crazy, I know. After all, if you're dead you're dead.

Anyway, there I was, lying naked on a rock at the edge of a lake whose name I didn't know. I closed my eyes against the sun. A light breeze skimmed my skin, moving the hair on my legs, belly and chest. I could feel the grit of sand grains between me and the cool granite and my skin took on a lazy glow from the sun. I heard the peaceful lap of wavelets on the shore and the sound of the breeze in the pines overhead. Birdsong, at least four or five different kinds, sprinkled the air. I slept.

A short time later I awoke, hungry and very thirsty. Scooping up cold lakewater, I gulped it greedily down. Soon I was dressed, with a full stomach, loading the canoe. I wanted out of that horrible place as soon as possible. I left my old clothing behind me and pushed out onto the calm lake in bright afternoon sunshine. I don't know why, but I felt *new*, as if this was the real start of my journey. Of course, I didn't know where I was going, but one thing I was sure of: I would sleep on islands from now on!

And late that afternoon I found an island on the same lake but hours of the Crabbe zig-zag farther on. It was shaped like a wedge—high on one end and tapering down to a nice little sand beach flanked with young birches.

When I had unloaded the canoe, beached it, turned it over and stored the paddles underneath, it was dusk. I turned and looked back down the lake to the other campsite but it was hidden by a point of land which jutted into the lake. Good. The sooner I forgot that place, the better.

I was pretty dragged out and decided to hit the sack early. Stars were beginning to show themselves in the darkening sky and there were no clouds. I figured I'd sleep out in the open. I found my bag, torn and still damp and soiled in a couple of places by vomit, climbed in, folding the dirty patches under, and fell asleep.

The sun woke me, already high in the sky. I put on a pair of shorts after washing in the lake and got to work. There was a lot to do.

First I unpacked everything. I laid out all the food—what seemed like an endless supply of cans—on the gravel near the water's edge. Next came my wardrobe—a small one now. Then all the equipment. I looked it all over. Everything was wet. Some of the equipment, like cooking pots, was dented from rough handling and bad packing. Cereal was leaking from squashed boxes.

I took a length of quarter-inch rope and strung it between two thick pines. I had to experiment with the knots so the line wouldn't droop. Then I hung up my clothes. The canvas packs, soggy and stiff, I hung from broken branches.

The tent was hauled into the lake for a good washing. It was ripped a little around the door and back wall but not too badly. I figured it would dry best if pitched so I did that. I got a pot of water to rinse the sleeping bag, dipping the dirty patches in, soaping them, rinsing again. That took ages, because I had to be careful not to get the down too wet. After spreading it over a low bush in the sun, I repacked the food in some sort of an organized fashion so the packs could be carried without giving me a hernia.

All this made me hungry. As the afternoon wore on, I began to picture and to taste a thick savory beef stew with rich brown gravy. But when I found the matches my vision disappeared. I had lots of matches all right—paper ones, fifty packets of paper matches. All soaking wet.

Dammit! I thought. And other worse words. My feeling of optimism disappeared in a cold wave. I grabbed a book of matches in desperation, ripped out a soggy match, tried to strike it alight. But the red sulphur match head crumbled; the sand on the striking patch was torn from the paper backing. It was useless.

For the first time, as I sat back on the pine-needled ground, I really wanted a drink. Where was Silent Sam when I really needed him? How good it would feel—to have him soothing me, dissolving the angles and edges from my anxiety and depression.

I ate cold, glutinous, sticky stew that night on a darkening beach, right from the tin. How could I go on without a fire? No heat. No cooking. (Not that I could cook worth a damn anyway.) No defence. Maybe I'd meet someone—a fisherman maybe—and borrow some. But I wanted to avoid people. That was the reason I was here in the first place.

I couldn't turn back. I just couldn't. To go limping home like a fool—the great outdoorsman, too stupid to waterproof his matches—I couldn't do it. I'd get too many "I told you so's" to count. I'd only confirm everybody's opinion that I needed them to run my life for me.

I would go on. After all, it was June, warm weather was coming, I could exist on cold food. I went to bed thinking, if I could survive that bear I could survive anything.

By noon next day I was on my way again, after a breakfast of raisin bran and lake water and cold instant coffee partially dissolved. I headed off.

Crabbe's Journal: 9

It's kind of embarrassing to admit this now, but you've probably already noticed that when I set out on my escape I had no idea where I was going. And I had no map or compass—which was logical in a way because I didn't know how to use either anyway.

But at the time I didn't know there was anything wrong or crazy in what I was doing. If I had thought about it, I'd have figured it was all pretty simple. For example, you go down a river, across a lake, throw in a few portages, and when you want to come home you just retrace your route. Easy, right? Wrong. When you recross, say, a lake, from the opposite direction, especially after a day or so, it looks like a different lake altogether. Everything—shoreline, shape of islands—looks different. So map and compass are essential.

But the thing about someone who is escaping is this: he's more concerned about what he's leaving than what he's going to. I was lost from the time I left Ithaca Camp. And what was worse, I didn't *know* I was lost.

So on I went that afternoon, looking for the river mouth where my father and I had gone fishing that long ago summer. It took a while to find it because there were several small bays at this end of the lake. It was shallow, about two canoe lengths wide, and had almost no current.

It was getting dusk by now, the air taking on a chilly dampness. I could see quick, dark birds darting along the water's surface and all sorts of chirrups and clunks were coming from the grasses in the bay.

I decided to camp there and get an early start in the morning. There was a small campsite at the river mouth so I headed for it, the marsh grass whispering as the canoe parted it. The shore was flat and the campsite was canopied and surrounded by dark evergreens. By the time I was set up it was almost dark. I went down to the shore-line to eat a can of cold pork and beans and look out over the narrow bay.

You know, people say that darkness falls, but it doesn't. I don't know how many times I've read that sentence—I do a lot of reading—"darkness fell." But, as I watched the shore which was covered with dense evergreens and the odd silver birch, I realized that darkness seems to *rise* from the floor of the forest, and as the sun sinks, the light seems to climb up the trunks as if to escape the blackness that wells up from the earth. Soon, only a few stars shone weakly, then disappeared behind the clouds that were moving in fast on the breeze.

I don't know how long I sat there—it was quite a while—before I noticed something else that surprised me. The forest is *noisy* at night. What's all this stuff about the quiet, nighttime woods? I could hear the breeze in the spruce branches, a loon laughing out on the lake, rustles, chirrups, frog-thunks, and other noises I didn't recognize.

And I'll tell you, after a while it got to me. I didn't feel so good. It was very dark—so dark that I could barely see the calm surface of the bay, protected by the trees from the night breeze—and the damp air chilled like a wet coat. I began to imagine all kinds of threatening sources for the noises I couldn't identify. Like insane killers who would invade my campsite and knife me with huge, curved blades, or another bear seeking to chew me up, or the same bear, come back to finish the job. Loneliness crept close, closer with each long, lonely "a-loooooooo" of the loon. Another Crabbe anxiety attack was on me, but not the kind I was used to. This was the same dread I had felt a few minutes before the bear came.

I got up and headed for the tent and my down womb. God, I wanted to talk to my old buddy, Silent Sam; the shivers that chilled me were not from the cold.

It was a long, fearful night. The kind that is supposed to build character but really just makes you want a drink and a sensible answer to the question, what the hell am I doing here? Or in the world, for that matter. It wasn't my first lonely night, I can tell you. But it had been a long time since I'd cried, and a long time since Sam was able to convince me that I didn't really need anybody.

There isn't much to tell about the next day. I got up as soon as I saw (gratefully) dawn's rosy fingers creeping over the horizon. The river travel was uneventful. I found a campsite on a small island that was much less gloomy than the last night's. But it rained and the plop and patter of drops on the fly increased my loneliness. I was also getting really jumpy. I have to admit Sam's absence had a lot to do with that. That night was the first time I seriously considered going home. I guess I got some sleep but not much.

It's funny how the weather affects you when you're living outdoors, though. A sunny day greeted me. It was warm, with a light breeze. The murmur of the river was background music to birdsong. I felt full of confidence: what the hell, so I had a few bad nights; I had lots of those at home.

So, after a continental breakfast of cold instant coffee and a couple of handfuls of Cheerios, intrepid Crabbe launched his loyal craft onto the bosom of whatever river it was.

For the first while I practiced my rudder technique, letting the current move me—which it did at a brisk rate, it seemed. It was like traveling down an artery at times because the forest came right to the edge of the water. Here, the river was only about twenty feet wide and fairly deep. Occasionally it would widen, trees would give way to a beaver pond. I saw a moose in one of these, staring at me with her long, stupid face, with weeds and whitish bulbs hanging dripping from her lips. Sometimes those bushes that looked sort of like blueberry bushes lined the river. If you were a science buff—which I wasn't then—you'd have had fits of delight over the variety of bushes and birds and stuff.

Until you began to hit the portages, that is. I began to encounter them about noon after I stopped for a munch. They were there to skirt the numerous little falls and rapids that started to show up. Although almost all the carry-overs were short—none over a hundred yards—they were difficult as hell, all mucky, strewn with boulders, sometimes pushing straight up an embankment and back down again a little farther on. I had to make three trips per portage. So, after a couple of hours I had lost most of my patience and all of my appreciation for the so-called beauties of nature. Some of the falls were really pretty, all laced with white foam, but at the time I hardly looked at them, just pressed on like a machine. It got so I groaned every time I heard the sound of fast moving water in the distance—a sound almost exactly like the wind in the tree tops.

I guess bone weariness mostly explains what happened. I wasn't paying too much attention to what I was doing and I was so whacked out I probably couldn't have got out of the mess anyway.

What happened was this: I'd just pushed off from a portage that ended below a chute of very fast, wicked looking water that snarled through a rock cut, tossing foam into the air. It wasn't registering with me that this river was getting quite a bit quicker and more treacherous, deeper and wider, as I struggled along, heaving packs or trying to keep the canoe straight in the swift current.

Anyway, I started off again and about fifty yards downstream from the portage was an almost right-angled bend in the river. I could hear loud roaring and figured it was the rapids behind me. Off I went, too tired to paddle, just steering. Then I noticed two things: I began to speed up and the river bottom seemed to leap toward me as it got shallow very quickly, so shallow I couldn't paddle even if I wanted to. I went lickety-split into that turn. And when I got into it the patented Crabbe paddling method failed me. The canoe began to revolve and the next thing I knew I was between two rock walls going like hell backwards down a fast chute, noise of water thundering in my ears. Sounds funny doesn't it, if you picture it? But when I turned around to look over my shoulder down the river, my heart stopped. The rock canyon I was trapped in narrowed quickly, like a long funnel, to end where two giant boulders squeezed the foaming river to no more than canoe length in width. And there the water just disappeared.

I was confused—for about five seconds. Then I got close enough to be shrouded in mist, spray, and the hellish roar of a falls. Over I went. And as I was suspended for a split second in mid air, you know what I thought? I thought, christ, Crabbe, I'll bet you look ridiculous! Can you believe it? For that microsecond before a very likely death I felt embarrassed!

But I didn't have time to blush. The stern of the canoe dropped crashing onto a boulder just beneath the surface and water, walls and ceilings of water smashed down on me. The packs rolled onto me, propelled by the rushing water, pounding the breath out of me. One of them bashed my arm against a gunwale and I felt a searing pain as the buckle slashed my forearm open. A second pack came square against my face and knocked me backwards into the pandemonium of leaping water. Then, as they say in the whodunits, everything went black.

WILLIAM BELL

But that was just the beginning. Two things—impressions—I remember: darkness and cold.

I've felt darkness and cold. Everybody has. But this wasn't the same. The dark was a dead, chilling liquid. And it was like I was slowly sinking into it, and it flowed into my ears and nose and mouth and filled me, dissolved me in blackness.

Cold is always white or blue, and it pinches you. But this cold was like the blackness. It invaded me, crept to the center, congealing like black slush. *It took me over,* turning my bones to dark ice.

And all the while, this sinking, forever, down and down. There was no fear, strangely enough, just the feeling that I had gone away.

Then the sinking stopped. The cold and darkness began to recede. Then—this is a little embarrassing—I had an erotic dream. A graceful woman walked naked from the sea and lay down with me, holding me firmly in her arms. She melted the cold away, now embracing me from the front, now from the back, and I could feel her life-warmth on my naked skin. Soon she went away, taking the darkness with her, and I lay in a warm cocoon.

I opened my eyes eventually. And there, above me, was the most beautiful face I had ever seen.

Crabbe's Journal: 10

She had large, gray eyes, full lips that were a little dry and cracked, and long, sandy-colored hair. Thinking I was still dreaming, I closed my eyes again.

"Come on. Try to sit up," said a human voice above me. "Come on."

Arms gripped me from behind and lifted me until I sat unsteadily. I rubbed my eyes and tried to hold them open. Bright sunlight made it difficult, shooting little arrows of pain onto my eyeballs. Finally, they focused on a woman, a tall, slender woman dressed in a red checked flannel shirt and jeans. She knelt in front of me and offered me a cup.

"Here. Drink."

I obeyed, still stupefied. I felt like I'd been asleep for a long time and I was completely disoriented. I drank down the delicious, warm soup. The more I swallowed the hungrier I got. Having drained the cup, I handed it back to her. She took it with rough, calloused hands, the nails short and a little dirty.

"Do you feel warm now?" she said, a little like an interrogator in her tone of voice.

"Yeah, I guess so."

"Well, think. Do you or don't you?"

"Yes, yes. I'm warm."

"Good. Count from one to ten."

"What?"

"Just do it," she commanded. Her voice was firm but not nasty—no cream puff, that's for sure. I counted, feeling a little silly.

"Okay, that's good." Her tone softened a little. "Now, gimme your name and where you're from."

I must have been fully to my senses by then because I balked at that one.

"No, I don't want to do that," I said.

"Why?"

"Just because I don't want you to know. I could make something up."

She smiled then and said, "You too, eh? Well that's okay. I just wanted to make sure your mind is working right. Hypothermia disorients the mind somewhat. You appear to be all right, though."

"What's 'hypothermia'?"

She sat back and crossed her long legs, Indian style, and rested her hands on her knees.

"When you went over the falls you almost drowned. The water in the river is very cold, and when I pulled you out you were already into shock. That's what hypothermia is, really, shock caused by the cold, which lowers your body temperature. Eventually, it will kill you. Disorientation of the mind is one of the symptoms."

"Oh," I said weakly.

She smiled.

"Sorry. Didn't mean to lecture. Want more soup?"

"Yes. Please. I'm awfully thirsty."

She got up and walked over to where a blackened pot sat balanced on a ring of rocks around a little, smokeless fire. What had she meant by saying, "You too, eh?" I wondered. She came back with more soup and handed me the cup.

"Thanks," I said. "This is good. What's in it?"

"Oh, let's see." She folded her long legs under her and sat down again. "Umm, fish heads, flour, some salt pork, lily roots, onions."

You might think I'd throw up at that description but that was the best soup I'd ever tasted. I was famished. It was hot, savory, full of tasty chunks of potato-tasting stuff.

"How did you find me?" I asked. "I don't remember anything after I went over." I had to shift my weight because I began to notice a pain in my chest, now that I was fully awake. Putting my hand to my ribs, I saw my left arm was bandaged from elbow to hand and splinted with two round, peeled sticks. Funny: as soon as I saw the dressing, which was bright blue flowery cloth, my arm began to throb.

"Careful," she warned. "You've got a couple of cracked ribs. I've bound your chest. That's why it's hard to get a deep breath. Is it very sore?"

I nodded.

"Your arm was cut pretty badly and it may be broken but I'm not sure. I splinted it just in case. To answer your question, I saw you go over the falls. I was down river a bit, putting out some night lines and I looked up just in time to see you disappear into the water. I thought you'd be dead by the time I got to you. It took me a while to fish you out of there, but everything seems to have worked out okay. I think you'd better go back to sleep, now. You've had a near miss and you need lots of rest."

"But I—" I wanted to thank her, to say something.

"We can talk later. There's lots of time."

I didn't argue because I could hardly keep my eyes open and I felt weak. So, handing her the empty cup I lay back and blanked out immediately.

When I woke again, I was lying on my back. I imagined I saw a great, blood-colored bird descending on me, and it terrified me until I realized I was looking up at a nylon fly that moved slowly, bellowed and was lifted rhythmically by the cool wind. I relaxed. My ribs and arm hurt slightly, like an engine throbbing in the background. I could hear the wind whistling in the trees around the campsite and every once in a while a crack or pop from the fire that glowed a dozen or so yards away.

Soon I became aware of breathing near me and realized the woman was asleep right beside me. I looked at her. She faced away from me, curled up. She was fully dressed, boots and all, and had a hat on, one of those knitted toques your mother tries to get you to wear. She slept like that, I assumed, because I was in her sleeping bag.

Who was she? I wondered. And what in hell was a beautiful woman doing way the hell and gone in the middle of nowhere? Was she alone? It seemed so. She knew what she was doing, unlike me, out here—one look at the campsite told me that. She could find and cook wild food; she knew first aid, did a really professional-looking job of fixing me up. And that face. A face that beautiful, you'd think, belonged in a classy drawing room or on the screen.

I looked at the thick hair that spilled from beneath her hat and thought that truth is stranger than fiction. There lay Crabbe, naked in a sleeping bag in the middle of nowhere, right beside a very attractive woman. Did I create fantasies from those ingredients? No. I rolled over, facing that friendly, comforting fire, and fell asleep.

The smell of the fire roused me to a morning already drenched in sunshine. I sat up in the bag (with difficulty), yawned and stretched as much as my ribs and sore arm would allow.

She was at the fire, frying something that sizzled deliciously and smelled the same, her back to me. Beyond her, a snowy mist hid the water and skirted the edge of the forest. A beautiful scene, peaceful, with no traffic honks and screeches, no mother screaming at you to get out of bed.

She turned and spoke in a voice that seemed to fit the scene.

"How do you feel this morning?"

"Fine, I guess. Still sore."

"Want to try to get up, then?"

"Not until I get my clothes."

She laughed and pulled my togs from a line she had strung between two birch saplings.

"I got most of the blood out," she said as she tossed them to me.

I dressed quickly, finding my boots beside the fire. They were dry and toasty. I felt a bit wobbly when I walked, but otherwise my body seemed in decent repair.

"You're just in time for grub," she said, and handed me a tin plate. There were two small fish, fried golden brown, and a chunk of bread that gave off a hot sweet odor that set my juices going. It was all delicious, washed down with strong, hot tea, strange tasting, but good. Later I found out it was Labrador tea she picked herself and dried.

We ate in silence. When I put down my plate and gulped the last of my second cup of tea, she ordered, "Let's see that arm."

I held it out for her while she untied the bright cloth strips that held the splints in place. Then she asked me to move my arm around, twist my wrist and so on. It hurt, but not badly.

"Good," she pronounced. "Not broken. I couldn't tell for sure when you were unconscious." She changed the dressing on the wound, an ugly slash across my forearm two or three inches above my wrist.

She poured two more cups of tea from the blackened tin can that served as her teapot. We sat there for a while, saying nothing, captured by the strange peacefulness of the fire, birdsong, and the wavelets at the shore, a small world under the huge, blue dome of the perfect sky.

The mist had been burned off by the morning sun, leaving the air clear and still. I looked around the tidy, homey campsite. Something I couldn't quite put my finger on struck me about the place. The two-person tent, clothes-lines, chopping block, and a little lean-to with gear in it were arranged in a wide semi-circle around the fireplace that was made up of the ring of stones and what I took to be a sort of oven affair also made of stones. We were about twenty yards from the water on a piece of land that rose gently from the bay—a sort of meadow fifty yards deep and thirty wide, carved out of the forest behind and sparsely treed with young white birch and spruce. There was a patch of sandy beach at the water's edge, but most of the shoreline was flat granite slab.

The campsite was on a little bay, edged with grasses, almost closed off from the main part of a lake that could be glimpsed through the two granite arms clothed with juniper scrub. Then I saw it: this place would be impossible to find from the main lake. Marsh grass grew across the gap—at this time of year, of course, what I saw was the dead stuff from last year and in the middle of summer it would be much thicker. The bay was like a secret harbor. Coincidence? Or had this strange, skillful woman chosen it for that reason?

"Now, suppose you tell me how it came about that you tried to shoot Trout Falls in a canoe, backwards."

Her words jarred me from my speculations. I said nothing for a minute, torn between the fear of letting my secret out and a sense of obligation to her. The peacefulness of the setting made me feel secure for some reason.

I figured in the end that I owed her an explanation: she *did* save my life, after all. But I wouldn't tell her everything.

I started my narrative at Ithaca Camp. And I left out my name.

The more I talked, the more unbelieving she looked. Occasionally she'd ask me a question and shake her head at the reply, but mostly she just let me talk. She was amazed that I just took off without really knowing where I was going and was totally shocked to learn I couldn't read a map or use a compass.

"It's already clear," she said almost snapping at me, "that you can't paddle a canoe."

I went on. I got a little miffed when she laughed about the bear attack. (I left out some of the results.)

"What's so goddam funny?" I said angrily. "I almost got killed!"

"Oh, I doubt that. The bear was rolling you around; it was curious to see if you had any more food—or if you *were* food." She giggled this time—*giggled* for God's sake. "If that old bruin wanted to hurt you, you'd be a mass of claw marks now. You were smart to roll into a ball and lie still."

"I wasn't smart at all. I was terrified and then I fainted."

"Yes, I know. It must have been horrible."

I searched her face to see if she was making fun of me. Her eyes were serious, sympathetic.

"But, you asked for it," she said.

"What the hell do you mean?" I shot back, not satisfied with her sympathy.

"Well, look: it's spring. Bears have been out of hiber- · nation for only a few weeks. They're hungry. And it's around mating season, so they're also bitchy. And the ones in that neighborhood are well used to humans. What do you do? Throw peanuts around, spill fish oil all over yourself, and leave candies in your tent. You invited every bear within miles to check you out! All you needed was a sign and an ad on T.V.!"

She laughed again. So did I. It was pretty stupid of me, come to think of it.

Then she stood up.

"Well, enough of this merriment. I've got to check the night lines."

"What are they?" I asked.

"It's a way of fishing without being there."

"Can I come?" Although I still felt weak and not really up to going anywhere, I didn't feel like being alone either.

"If you like," she said casually. She started walking toward the water. There was a little copse of black spruce right at the shore to the left of the beach and from it she lifted a sixteen foot, cedar-strip canoe and placed it in the water, neat as you please. This was no weak woman, I'll tell you. She handed me a paddle.

"Put this at your feet. Don't try to paddle; you're too weak. In you get."

In I got, after she showed me how to do so properly. She shoved off and we headed out of the bay, across the open water then through the marsh grass at the gap. Once out, I turned and looked back toward the campsite. I had been right: the place was invisible.

We were in a decent sized lake and to the left of us, a river, called the North, entered it. We moved upriver, past the dense spruce forest that marched right to the shore. The deep water reflected the flawless sky.

And I'll tell you. That woman could handle a canoe. After twenty minutes of swift, *straight* progress we got into strong current. The water got shallower and occasionally a menacing boulder stuck a finger into the air. But she just took that boat exactly where she wanted to go.

The roaring of Trout Falls came upon us suddenly as we rounded a bend. We moved slowly now, but steadily, and finally entered a small pool at the foot of the cascading water. She manoeuvred us toward a little sand beach where the powerful current backed up on itself and left a calm spot. We, me with one arm, pulled the boat up onto the sand.

The Falls was about twenty yards across the turbulent pool and about eight yards high. Don't get me wrong: I'm not saying it was Niagara or anything. And it was quite narrow because of those big boulders up top that squeezed the river thin. But—it's hard to describe the feeling of naked power and energy it conveyed as the tons of water leapt to crash in a boiling rage onto the black boulders scattered around the base. The woman said that the pool was incredibly deep and a vicious tangle of opposing currents.

She showed me where she had pulled me out and pointed to what was left of my canoe—a shapeless mass of smashed red fiberglass jammed between two boulders around which angry water boiled and churned. The packs were at the bottom of the pool somewhere.

I'll tell you, I stared at that scene with my mouth hanging

open for a long time. How on earth had I survived *that?* I asked her how she had fished me out. Very matter of factly, no bragging, like she was writing a newspaper report, she pointed here and there and described the events, how she had got me out, carried me to this beach, taken me home.

"It's a good thing the current is strong," she said. "It pushed you to a relatively quiet spot of water and I was able to get to you."

I thought about it—hard—while she told it, tried to picture the whole thing. She must be incredibly strong, tough and brave, I thought. She risked her life for me. She brought me back into the world. I stared at her in awe.

"Don't look at me like that," she said, embarrassed, I guess. "It's no big deal. You'd have done it for me or someone else." And then she headed toward her night lines.

No, I wouldn't, I said to myself. I wouldn't have done it for anybody. I followed her, ashamed.

Crabbe's Journal: 11

We spent an hour or so checking the lines, removing the fat little speckled trout from the hooks, and resetting them. She had a weight on one end of each line, from which six or eight shorter lines dangled, with a baited hook on each. She'd toss the whole contraption out into the current and tie the free end to a strong stick jammed into the sand. The trick was to set the line in such a way that it didn't tangle or get swept downstream.

On the way back to the campsite we made better time, being with the current. I got a good view of the lake from that direction as we left the rivermouth, but I couldn't find the campsite. She could.

After we got back, she showed me the wonderfully interesting job of gutting the fish. What fun that was, blood and insides all over my hands, surrounded by unhappy looking fishheads and white entrails. just as I threw all that stuff into the lake and washed the slime and blood off my hands, she served up the "grub" as she called it: bread, tea, and some tiny wild strawberries that tasted wonderful—not like those fat red blobs you get in the supermarket. She called the bread "bannock" and cooked it by packing the heavy dough around a peeled stick, jamming the other end between the fireside rocks and letting the sausage-like thing rest just above the coals. It cooked up steamy and aromatic and delicious.

After lunch I got her mad at me. She wanted to change the bandage on my arm again and sent me to the lean-to at the edge of the trees to get some clean rags out of a pack while she mixed up more dough for supper. Not having listened too well to her directions, I fumbled with the buckles and straps of the first pack I laid eyes on. I just got the top flap open—it was one of those big canvas packs like I had—when she screamed. I mean, she didn't just yell; she shrieked like a banshee.

"Get the hell out of there! What do you think you're doing?"

She shot across that clearing like a crazy hornet and slapped my hands away violently, sending spears of pain up the wounded arm.

"Get away! Don't you *ever* go into this pack! Do you hear? Do you?" Her red face was contorted with anger.

"Y-yes," I stuttered. "I'm sorry; I..." Stepping backwards, clutching my aching arm, I caught a heel on a root and fell back, squatting heavily on my rear end and driving the air from my lungs with a whoosh. My ribs began to throb as I gasped for breath. I must have groaned.

Looking over her shoulder at me as she buckled up the pack she said, "I'm sorry," in a more normal tone. She took the rags from a small duffle bag and said, "Come over to the fire and I'll redress that arm."

She would not look at me as she did so.

"There's very private...stuff...in that pack. You must promise me you'll never look into it."

She spoke in an embarrassed tone but there was no mistaking the fact that I had to promise. So I did.

"Sure. Yeah, I promise." I wouldn't cross *this* woman! I'd never survive.

I spent the next couple of weeks or so not doing much of anything, just lazing around the campsite mostly, doing little, odd jobs for her. I slept a lot. Nightmares visited me once in a while—bears chasing me over waterfalls of vodka I tried to drink but couldn't—and I woke up sweating and screaming occasionally. The woman talked to me for a few minutes and I'd fall back asleep. The urge to visit Silent Sam was kind of strong sometimes.

I would putter around the campsite, trying to learn to make bread and brew decent tea and build a proper cooking fire (you make it small, using softwood for a fast, hot fire for tea; or with hardwood which you let burn down to coals for a hot, long-lasting fire). If I felt spunky, the woman took me up to the Falls or for a long walk into the bush where she checked and set snares for rabbits on the edge of a swamp.

After I mastered bread and tea and fires, I graduated to the important task of tending the smoke fire. Not a fire that smokes—a fire to smoke meat, to prepare it for storage. She showed me how to cut the head off a trout, slit it open from gills to tail, gut it, take out the gills, then press it flat and lay it on a little rack made of green sticks that leaned over the tiny, smoky fire. After a few hours, the fish turned leathery and tasted like—you guessed it—fish and smoke. The rabbit meat was cut into thin strips and draped over the same rack. It took longer to dry to a brittle consistency, dark brown. It tasted like wood. She called it jerky. Because the meat and fish were fully dried, they could be stored for a long time. A neat trick.

"How come you want to store all this food?" I asked her one day as I was slicing up more rabbit.

"For the winter. Can't rely on snares to keep me in grub. I also have to dry some berries and tubers so—"

"Winter?" I interrupted. "You're going to stay all winter?"

"Stayed last winter."

"Jumpin' Jesus!" I exclaimed—one of my favorite expressions, except around my parents, who go to St. James' Anglican Church, religiously so to speak. Except most of the religion leaks back out of them before they get home.

"Which reminds me," the woman continued, "you've been here long enough to begin to trust me, so I think we'd better have a long chat." And she sat in her I'm-going-to-relax pose.

That was a joke. I was to trust *her*, but she had taken that pack into the bush and hidden it the day after I'd opened it by mistake.

"What do you want to talk about?" I said, sitting down, Indian style, across the smoke fire from her.

"Well, for one thing, I don't know your name. For another, we have to get you back home sooner or later. Not that I don't enjoy your company; but you can't stay here forever."

"When are *you* leaving?" I asked.

"I don't know," she said. A veil seemed to drop between us as her voice took on a bit of an edge. She tried to hide it, but she was becoming guarded.

"But when *I* leave has nothing to do with you."

"Why not?" I could play this game, too. "By the way, I don't know *your* name either."

We danced around like this for a while. It was kind of amusing, really; each circling the other, waiting, hoping the other would go first.

Finally, she laughed—a rich, friendly laugh that dissolved the barrier of mistrust between us.

"All right, all right. You win. My name is Mary Pallas."

"I'm Franklin Crabbe. Please call me Crabbe. I hate the other name. Pleased to meet you." And I reached across the smoke rack, holding out my hand. She took it in a firm, bloody grip.

"Charmed, I'm sure." She laughed again. "Come on, Crabbe. I'll make some tea."

So we sat around the fire while a stew simmered in the pot for supper. I told her everything. Why not, I figured. If you can't trust the woman who saved your life, who can you trust? I meant to hold some back but once I got rolling it all came out—everything—and the longer I talked, the more bitter it got. I knew that.

I knew I sounded like a moaner, but it kept coming. Mary, the warm, sunwashed June day, the light breeze off the lake, the savory aroma of the stew, all worked together to soak out the poison. And everybody got slashed in my narrative, my teachers, my "friends," especially my parents, especially them. By the time I wound down, I was sobbing. And that's something because I've *never* cried in front of another human being since I was three.

"You see?" I concluded, wiping my eyes with an embarrassed hand, "I've got nothing to go back to—nothing and nobody. What the hell's the point?"

It was a measure of her wisdom, a quality I got to know and rely on as time passed, that Mary never contradicted this statement. Most people would have started to hand out advice, piling up clichés like old newspapers. But she just said, "You're a very bitter man, Crabbe."

"How can you say I'm a man, sitting here snivelling like a baby?"

"Now that's the first really dumb thing you've said since you began your autobiography," she said. Mary was nothing if not blunt. "Come on, that stew's about ready."

I felt a lot better after supper—full, warm, and calm. It was dark by then. A good moon was rising and a cool, brisk breeze swept through the campsite, taking the smoke off at a sharp angle. We sat talking for a long time, our conversation full of long silences.

Finally I said, "Mary?"

"Yes, Crabbe?"

"You don't have to tell me anything. It doesn't matter. I understand, I think." I paused for a moment. "And I'll leave if you want."

Mary put down her cup and leaned forward intently. "Crabbe, I can't tell you much. It's not a matter of trust;

it's just better if you know nothing about me. I'll tell you this much: I've run away too. It's very, very important that *nobody* finds out I'm here. I've been here a year now and I'm staying the winter. After that...I don't know. I just don't know."

"But don't you get lonely—and *bored*?"

She picked up a little stick and stirred the coals sending little showers of red ash up. "Bored? Never. Lonely? Of course. That's why I'd like you to stay for a while, if you want."

I almost jumped up and kicked my heels.

"You bet I would!"

Conscious that I sounded like a five-year-old with a new Christmas toy, I shut up.

Silently, she got up and went over to the tent, returning with a couple of warm shirts, for the night was growing chilly. She took up her position across from me. It's funny, you know, how a fire will weld people together, as if the leaping flames and the warmth go to your heart.

So when she asked, from nowhere, "Do you find it hard, Crabbe, living without the liquor?" I just answered her as if she'd just asked for the time.

"Yes," I said. "I get bitchy and full of anxiety. It comes in spells. Christ, I'm glad I wasn't deeper into it. I'm almost an alcoholic." (That was a greater confession than it sounds.)

"What a bloody useless character I am," I added and looked into the fire, shame welling up from inside.

"Don't feel sorry for yourself, Crabbe. Guilt is just another form of escape."

My anger jumped, but I said nothing. She was right, so why argue? Guilt is another escape and so is self-pity. And so is booze.

Although I was terrifically pleased that I'd been asked to stay, I felt empty and a little afraid when I sacked out—as if, if I could open up my head and look into myself I'd see only empty space, a shred of darkness wrapped in skin. Layer by layer I was being stripped away: the ordeal with the bear; the waterfall; my breaking down tonight and admitting what I never before admitted to anyone, including myself. What would happen, I wondered, when the last layer was peeled off? What would be left?

Crabbe's Journal: 12

I've been going to school all my life, like most people, but I learned more from Mary than in all those years put together. Useful things too—not the accusative case or parabolas or 1867 or metaphors. Growing up in the city, I had a very idealistic attitude toward old Ma Nature, like: the wilderness is a beautiful, peaceful place, populated with cute little birds and noble animals. Well, that's bunk. So is the opposite notion, that Nature is a monster-mother full of traps and vicious violence. The truth is, Nature is just *there.* All those cute little beings survive by eating other beings. On the other hand, you don't need to think of the wilderness as a horrible threat waiting to gobble you up either. It's the way it is and that's that. You can't change it by wishful thinking or complaining.

And I grew to like that fact after a while. Everything I learned from Mary was useful. When you live in the bush, everything you do is *significant,* it *means something,* because, if you don't know what you're doing or you're not careful, you get wet or drowned or hungry or lost. Something will happen to you, that's a certainty. Nature isn't nasty. It is what it is and you're part of it. You aren't in control like you are in the city. You work *with* the environment not against it. Like a sailor. He doesn't fight the wind, he works with it. And he can't do that until he learns about it.

In the city, nothing I did *mattered.* If I left my clothes lying around, somebody picked them up. If I forgot my raincoat I called a cab. I left my calculator on the subway once; I just bought a new one at the nearest store.

But out there in the bush, as I said, everything mattered, and I learned that fast. Sure, life meant a lot of hard work, but if things are important you get a feeling of satisfaction when you do them well.

A few days after our long talk, Mary and I were back in the bush setting some snares in an area she had never tried before. I walked along behind her watching her slim, lithe figure move gracefully through the sun-shot hardwood bush. She walked in long, easy strides, her sand-colored hair swinging back and forth across her back. From time to time she stopped, checked her compass, turned and looked in the direction from which we'd come, then moved on, her boots barely rustling the dry leaves on the forest floor. Presently the land sloped and we approached copses of spruce and cedar and the ground was wet in patches.

We set snares for an hour or so. When the last one had been carefully arranged, Mary straightened up, wiped her hands on her pant legs and looked at me, smiling. Her gray eyes looked mischievous.

"Okay, Crabbe," she said nonchalantly, "lead us home."

"Oh, yeah. Right. Sure."

"No, really," she said, all innocence. "Take us back. Which way, Leader?"

"Haven't got a clue."

She then leaned against a windfall.

"What would you do if I weren't here. If we got separated?"

I answered, "Oh, I don't know. Let's see. First I think I'd panic for a few minutes. Then scream. Then run around like a chicken with its head cut off. Then call a cab."

She laughed.

"Okay, come on." And off she went trailed by her faithful follower.

That night, right after a supper of fish soup and bannock, we started compass school. And the next day, in a fine drizzle, Mary took me for a long walk in the greening woods and we practiced taking bearings. It's pretty easy. The tricky part is taking the bearing and then staying on course over uneven ground and around obstacles—like swamps, for instance.

After a week I could lead us into the bush and back with only a few corrections from Mary. I also learned a little about "reading" the terrain. Mary claims that if you live somewhere long enough you get familiar with the bush just like you get used to the buildings and streets of a city.

I was amazed to find that you can use a map and compass to find out where you are if you are lost—where on the map, I mean. You use a process called triangulation, with some sharp eye-work and a little arithmetic. We even did it by drawing a map in the dirt.

Then, one sunny morning after breakfast Mary announced in that out-of-the-blue way of hers, "I think today's the day."

She looked up at the sky, made a big show of looking around the campsite.

"Yup. No rain tonight, no pressing work to do. It's a good day for it."

"Yeah, you're right. Definitely," I said. I was used to the way Mary would say something with no connection to what you had been talking about. As if you'd been in her head all along, listening to her thoughts.

"A great day for the Big Test," she continued. She stood and clapped her hands together.

"Come on, Crabbe, exam time. Grab your bedroll, a knife, canteen and some matches. Wrap up that lump of bannock."

"I'm not moving," I answered casually, and poured myself some tea. I lay back on one elbow. "You have clearly gone insane."

"Aren't you F-period Crabbe, school wonderboy, great scholar?" Her eyes were wide in mock wonder.

"You got it. That's me. And you are a crazy goddess, talking in riddles."

"Well, today you prove that compassing is one of your many accomplishments. So move your butt."

Half an hour later we were on the other side of the lake, standing on the tiny beach there. The sun still shone warmly and the merest ripple could be seen on the lake.

"Turn around," Mary commanded.

I don't know if you've ever been led, blindfolded, through the bush: believe me, it's an experience. Mary led me for what seemed an eternity and finally stopped.

"Sit." I sat. The blindfold came off. After squinting against the light for a minute, I looked around. I was sitting on a large boulder in the middle of the bush. Of course, I recognized nothing. Suddenly I felt very uneasy: it had just occurred to me that only *I* had brought a bedroll.

"Mary, I—"

"Don't talk, Crabbe. Listen. Take this."

She handed me a piece of birch bark (how pioneerish, I thought) with writing on it, and her compass.

"Read that later. It has bearings and directions on it. Now, follow the directions *exactly.* I mean, precisely. Got it?"

"Yeah, right. Exactly." I wondered if she noticed the tension in my voice.

"And," she paused dramatically to get my attention, "if you come across water, you've screwed up. Stop and make a smoky fire and stay put. Repeat that."

"Knock off the drama, Mary. I heard you."

She just looked at me till I repeated it all.

"But where am I *going,* Mary? Back to the beach?" "You didn't listen, Dopey. If you get back to the beach, you've screwed up!"

"But—"

"Never mind. Do as I say. Follow your first instruction."

I read the bark. "Sixty degrees to big pine. Don't look back." That was it.

Off I went, fighting the urge to look over my shoulder and say something to her. I lasted about fifty yards then turned to see her. She had disappeared.

Mary had set up the trial so that I would have to spend

the night in the bush and I realized after I'd spent most of the day following her directions that I wasn't going to get off easily. I had some moments of doubt too. She had said to me a million times, "Trust the compass, Crabbe." Because many times I felt like I *knew* where to go but the compass didn't agree. It was the same now, but I doggedly maintained my faith in the magic window with the needle in it. Basically I made out all right.

It was what *else* was going on in my head that gave me trouble. On one level I was very logical—following the directions and bearings as exactly as I could, making decisions about the landmarks. But below the calculations, like a dark, damp room in the basement under the computer banks, I was getting very uneasy: the farther I went, the deeper I traveled into the bush alone.

This was different from water travel. There, you move through open space. The sky is right there, over you; you are comforted by the horizon. And you can see where you've come from, how far you've traveled.

But the bush, waiting quietly in the shore of every lake, the bush is different. Even in spring, when the buds are beginning to unfurl, it swallows you down. The trees crowd you and the sky is distant, held from you by millions and millions of strong branches. You walk and walk, growing more and more fatigued, sweaty and irritated as you slip and stumble or get slashed across the eye by the whip-like branch of a sapling. Swamps and bogs, dark, wet, and even more crowded, threaten you and cause time-consuming detours. And no matter how many hours you travel, you have almost no sense of progress. Not until you reach terrain that you recognize, if you reach such terrain at all.

I didn't. I didn't know *where* I was going or when I would get there. And there was always the chance that I wouldn't get there at all.

So by the time the forest began to darken and I spread my bedroll on a bed of piled up leaves on a piece of flat ground in the lee of a rock out-cropping, I was very tired and very uneasy. "Fear" isn't the right word, although fear was a part of it. I don't know if you've ever felt totally isolated, but that's sort of what it was like. There was, literally, no one but me there—out in the middle of nowhere.

As I lay rolled up in old blankets, settled in for the long wait for dawn, I thought a lot about loneliness. How I sometimes felt alone in a crowd of other kids, in the school gym at an assembly The Beet called for some stupid reason like a pep rally, American style, for the football team. How I went through my day with no real friends. How our formal dinners at home were three people "in solitary," condemned, it seemed, forever. How my life was symbolized by a mental picture I carry around in my head: a teenager alone in his room, staring into the T.V. screen, hating whatever program is on, sipping on vodka, waiting for sleep.

And how it was mostly my fault. Oh, I like to blame them, blame them all. But it was me.

Nice way to spend the night in the bosom of Ma Nature, eh? I lay there all night, trying to figure the answer. Was my life very different from others'? Were we *all* alone, in spite of the illusion of comfort from other people? Or was

I only depressed by the dark, alien bush that wrapped me like a cloak?

By the time the bush was filled with soft gray light I was sitting up with my back to a big sugar maple. Naturally I had no answer to those questions, and naturally they seemed less urgent with the return of dawn. Who does have an answer, though? All I knew was that my loneliness was mostly my own fault.

It was very hot by late afternoon. My shirt was glued to me. Grimy and bitchy, I sat down on a huge fallen oak that Mary had chosen for a landmark—the last landmark on the list of instructions she'd given me. I chewed hungrily on some bannock, took a pull on the canteen, and tried to ignore the few black flies that the heat had brought out.

"About time you got here."

It was Mary's voice. My head snapped back and forth. I stood up and spun around. I couldn't see her.

"Where are you?" I demanded, trying to keep the sound of relief from my voice.

She stood up, not six feet from me. She'd been lying among a clutch of maple saplings.

"Right here, Crabbe. You all right?"

"Yeah, I'm fine. Nice to see you. I missed you," I blurted.

"Well, well, well," she said, half seriously. "Do you know that's the first time you've admitted to a positive emotion since I met you?"

I smiled. "Yeah, well. I feel pretty good today, I guess."

As she turned and began to walk through the hardwoods she said over her slender shoulder, "Tell me."

"Tell you what?" I walked along beside her. Our feet rustled the dry leaves.

"Tell me how you feel, dummy."

"Oh, well, I don't know—sort of proud, I guess. Like I did something good."

"You *did* do something good, Crabbe. That was a tough route I worked out for you. I won't ask you if you were scared because I know you were. I would have been. By the way, you were safe all the time. I had you working back and forth on a big peninsula. So even if you went off course you'd have hit water and I could get you out."

We came out of the bush—right onto the little beach we were at yesterday. I had ended up a hundred yards from where I'd started. That didn't surprise me.

"So all the time," I said, a little disappointed, "that I was sweating about going off course and wandering up to the bloody North Pole, I was in a big, leafy playpen, safe as a baby?" I wasn't mad. But my feeling of pride was gone.

"Yes, you were safe. But you didn't *know* that, Crabbe. Don't miss the point. Your accomplishment was the same. *You* did it. Now the forest needn't be a terrible mystery to you." She handed me a paddle and we lifted the canoe into the water. "You don't have to be blind any more," she added. "And listen, Crabbe, if you've got a good reason to feel good about yourself—and you do—then *do* it. You don't need anybody's permission."

Before we had paddled halfway across the lake I felt good again. Living with her was like that.

Crabbe's Journal: 13

That first month or so was pretty rough. Oh, I don't mean the work or the demands Mary made on me to learn skills that would raise me to a notch above "useless" on the evolutionary scale. Mostly, I enjoyed that part. And I wasn't, as you might think, having problems controlling my animal urges with this beautiful woman around. I *had* them, I'm not saying I didn't, but Mary didn't come on like the women on T.V.—either syrupy smiles, big fluttery eyes, and an air of helplessness, or more manly than a truckdriver (to prove she was liberated)—no, she was just Mary. Hell, I was the helpless one, not her.

The real problem was that I was still having trouble getting along without my "pal," Silent Sam. It wasn't easy, stopping dead like that, and I don't know what made me think that I wouldn't need it when I ran away. I never really lost the desire for a talk with Sam during the day—it was a bit like a slow burn. But once or twice, usually if it was in the afternoon and usually if I was taking a break, I'd really get the craving. I'd get jumpy and bitchy and lose all my patience. This state would pass after a while.

Mary was pretty good about it. She picked up pretty quickly on what was happening and began to watch for my bad moments. She would often suggest we do something distracting like go for a swim or have a canoe lesson or go pick wildflowers along the ancient, disused railway line about a mile away. I'm ashamed to say I told her to bugger off and leave me alone a few times.

One evening after supper I was washing up the "dishes"— cans, tin plates, bush knives, porcelain-covered tin cups— while Mary sat sipping Labrador tea. She'd been quiet for quite a while and I recognized the look. Her graceful brows would tense up, her eyes seemed to go out of focus, and she'd tap the end of her nose with her right forefinger.

"What's up?" I said, more to break the silence than anything.

"Ummmmmm?" She looked up. Her eyes locked in again. "I think I have an idea, Crabbe. Yup. It might just help."

And, standing, she turned on her heel and walked casually across the campsite into the bush.

I knew where she was headed, too. To that big pack she kept hidden from me. The mystery bag.

She returned with something in her hand and resumed her favorite seat on the log by the fire.

"Here, take this," she said, holding something out to me.

It was a pipe, with an apple-shaped bowl and a short stem, maybe five inches.

My father smokes a pipe. He has eight thousand or so of the damn things—probably thinks they improve his corporate image—and he's forever stuffing the bowl, lighting, tamping, relighting, coughing, and blowing sweetish "aromatic" smoke all over the house. He never seems to get the knack of keeping the thing lit and so is always in the process of lighting rather than smoking. Racks of pipes litter the house: clay ones, wood ones, white, brown, yellow, even a *red* one for godsake.

But this little pipe that Mary handed me across the fire was different. Not one bit of it was without carving. And I don't mean elk's heads or elephant feet or any of that crap. On the front of the bowl was a circle bisected horizontally by a curved line, like a stretched out "S." It looked sort of like this:

Around the circle were lines organized into little squares. The rest of the bowl and stem were covered with lines and leaves, all curled and twisting in and out, over and under, so that if you followed a line with your finger you could never find the beginning or the end. It was beautiful, delicate yet strong.

I held it, lightly tracing the lines, waiting for Mary to speak.

"I'm not sure about this idea I've got, Crabbe. God knows smoking is almost as stupid a habit as drinking." Her soft voice drifted across our little fire in the waning light. Still fascinated with the designs, I didn't look up.

"But," she continued, after half a minute, "maybe when you really want a drink, you could light up that pipe and it would take your mind off Whatshisname."

"Silent Sam."

"Yes, Silent Sam. If you're careful not to inhale the smoke, perhaps you'll find it easy to break the habit once you don't need it any more. Think it's worth a try?"

"I don't know. I've got nothing to lose."

"Okay, here." She handed me a flat tin. Balkan Pride tobacco.

"I've got more of that if you need it."

"How come you—"

She cut in quickly, "Never mind. Let's have another cup."

Recognizing I was on the edge of forbidden territory, I shut up. We took our tea down to the bay shore and sat in our usual spot on the granite shelf by the little beach. The light was fading quickly now over our shoulders and night noises were beginning to swell. Bats flitted out over the calm waters of the bay that reflected the darkening shadows of trees on the shoreline.

Mary told me about the pipe. It had been made in China at least fifty years ago, carved by hand from the best briar in the world. Then polished and polished and polished with a special oil. That's what gave it the curious patina, she explained. The carving was all very symbolic. The circle, she said was something called a yin-yang symbol. It expressed a certain basic philosophy of life and existence that emphasized the unity of life and the harmony of inner peace. Or something like that. I couldn't quite follow her explanation. She talked on long after it got completely dark. It was the longest speech I had ever heard her make and I was content to try to understand all the very deep stuff she was telling me while my fingers traced the lines on the pipe. After a while I tried smoking it and managed fairly well for my first time.

And I couldn't help but wonder where Mary got all this knowledge she was pouring out on the dark, peaceful shore of our hidden bay. She knew a lot. She was dropping names I'd never heard of. I figured she must be university educated. And what she was saying—it wasn't the kind of rambling, shapeless talk you'd hear from most people. It was organized, as if she'd done this before. I looked at her as carefully as I could in the dark. She was with me and somewhere else at the same time.

But the way she talked about the pipe in particular, I knew it was precious to her. Although I didn't know why. I guessed it had belonged to somebody she loved.

And she had given it to *me*. Worthless old Crabbe. I didn't think her idea would work, to tell you the truth. But if she was willing to invest something of value to her on me, I was certainly willing to try.

It worked pretty well, as it turned out—that and the passage of time. Once I got the knack of keeping the thing lit

I enjoyed it. When the craving for a talk with Sam came upon me, pinching like an irritating iron caliper on my brain, I'd stop whatever it was that I was doing, stuff the bowl with that weird smelling tobacco, light up and puff away gently. Smoking sort of relaxed me. A special mood came with it. And sometimes when we two were hiking out to check the snares or pick berries I'd just hold the pipe in my hand, running my thumb over the design as we strode along. The wilderness and those never-ending hand-carved lines had a special effect on me.

Crabbe's Journal: 14

Once I sort of fit into our way of life out there, the days melted and ran together. We lived in a gentle rhythm. To bed with the sun and up with the sun, or maybe a little earlier on a nice morning to watch the dawn come spreading over the hills and across the lake like red-gold syrup. There were days when I forgot where I'd come from. And of course I refused to think about the future, even when the weather began to turn a little colder.

I grabbed a little self-respect out of those days too. I was in good shape for the first time ever. I could walk at a good pace all day through the bush. The canoe no longer bullied me on a portage; I flipped it onto my shoulders just like they do in the movies and shuffled along, one arm dangling, the other balancing the craft. I was strong. My limbs felt light and supple. I ate like a starved army.

Better still, I got so I actually thought I could survive in the bush without Mary—on an elementary level—able to find food (vegetable, animal and fish), build shelter, make fires (even in the pouring rain), cook fairly edible meals. I filed away lots of names for the thousands of living things around me. Of course, I was just beginning to tap the huge well of Mary's knowledge, and winter would soon send me packing toward civilization.

I knew I'd turned a corner in my struggle with Silent Sam too. I was healthier and the craving came less often and more mildly. And I was bugged more by curiosity than the desire for booze. The mystery pack: it contained answers to the millions of questions I had about Mary. I was sure of that. But just as I feared her angry silence if I asked the wrong questions, I knew that tampering with that pack would kill our relationship. So I tried to put my curiosity behind me. It was tough, though. Because I wanted more and more to know about her, who she was, where she'd come from, what her dreams were, what she thought of me. Especially that last part. I wanted her to respect me. More than that, I wanted in the worst way for her to love me. Because I realized one sunny day as I sat on the shore watching her swim, gracefully moving her long, golden limbs through the clear water, I loved her.

Crabbe's Journal: 15

The first frost of the year surprised me. When I emerged from the tent one morning at dawn (it was my turn to start the fire and make the tea) the whole campsite was coated with what looked like frozen mist. As soon as the sun cleared the horizon the frost quickly turned to moisture, but as the wood caught fire I thought about the time of year and it seemed that the days *were* a little shorter, the lake water *was* chilly—almost too cold for comfortable swimming—and we wore heavier clothing these days.

Soon the trees traded in their many shades of green for the colors of autumn: bright yellow on the birches and poplars, flaming red and orange on the hardwoods, blood red on the sumacs. Later still, after the cold began to pinch the leaves from the branches, cold, bitter rains fell from leaden skies and chevrons of geese and ducks were on the move. Some rafted up out on the main lake at night.

One morning we were sitting in the tent waiting out a miserably cold drizzle. That morning there had been ice on our bay shore.

"Crabbe," said Mary, after sitting in her thinking pose for a while, "I think it's time."

"Naw," I replied, misunderstanding her, "still raining to beat hell out there."

"Umm? No, no, I mean it's time we planned your re-entry into civilization." She hunched her shoulders, gathering her sleeping bag tighter around her.

A sinking feeling went through me. I knew this was it—I had been expecting it. It had snowed several days before, melting when it hit the ground and snow must have triggered her thoughts too.

I stuffed my hand in my pocket for my pipe, and I said, trying not to sound whiny and pleading like a child, "I don't want to go, Mary."

I cleared my throat, looked into those gray eyes, and called up all the courage I could, all the persuasiveness I could.

"Mary, I know you won't like this, but I have to say it. I love you. I want to stay with you. I don't want to go back."

She began to speak but I jumped from a sitting position to my knees, my sleeping bag falling away, and took her shoulders in my hands and rushed on.

"I've got nothing to go back to, really. I'm telling the truth. You know that. I don't want to leave you here. *You're* where I want to be."

And her gray eyes slowly filled with tears as she sat silently. The water magnified the gray for a moment then the tears overflowed and ran down her cheeks.

"I knew this would happen," she said in a small voice that seemed to come from somewhere else. "I knew I shouldn't have kept you here. I'm sorry Crabbe. It's just that I was so lonely."

"Don't be. Don't be sorry. Look, isn't there another way? Couldn't you—couldn't you come with me?"

"No," she whispered. "Impossible."

We were silent for a moment. The rain pattered sharply on the tent.

"Crabbe?" she said finally. "You have to go. You see that don't you?"

"Yeah, I see that."

"And thanks for what you said," she continued. "I love you too. You're a fine man."

It's strange. The way she said that, I knew she didn't mean romance love, the kind I felt for her. She meant a friend's love, and that was almost better. Romances seem to come and go nowadays, but good friends stay that way. So I was filled with fighting feelings: sadder than I've ever been that I had to finally go; happier than I've ever been that she loved me, the person I wanted most in the world to love me.

So I didn't say anything. I moved my hands from her shoulders and hugged her. She held me tightly for a long time and we both cried. It was a corny scene, I guess, if you weren't involved.

Two days later we began what was to be our last trek together. We headed out on a chilly but sunny morning and had to break through a thin layer of ice on the surface of the bay until we got to the main lake.

You'd never guess where we were going. We were on a raid. That's right, a raid. Not kid stuff, either. This was for real.

Mary's plan, as usual, was sensible with a little touch of craziness thrown in. We were out of staples like salt, flour and stuff like that (mainly because my presence in the household made the food go twice as quickly). I wondered one day where we'd get more and that led to wondering where my companion had got the stuff we were using.

"I stole it," Mary said casually.

"What? You ripped off a Miracle Mart?" I laughed. She laughed too. We hadn't been doing much of that lately.

"No," she continued, "from a hunt camp. Just a minute."

She took a quick trip into the bush and returned lugging the mystery pack and plunked it down by the fire. Pulling the leather straps free, she took out a map and spread it out on the ground. She knelt down and so did I.

"I guess I can show you where you are now, since you're leaving," she said.

The map showed in detail the whole area where we were situated. Mary pointed out our lake, the bay where our homesite was hidden away from the world. Thanks to my newly gained map-reading ability I was able to trace my route from Ithaca Camp. (What an idiot I had been.)

Mary also pointed out why this was a good place to hide. There were no roads for miles and miles—not even logging tracks. And no canoe routes came through the area, mainly because of the dangerous nature of the rivers that entered and exited our lake.

"See this square dot?" She indicated with her finger near the bottom, almost off the map. "This is the hunt camp. It's about four hundred yards from this medium-sized lake that's part of a chain of lakes. They're just off the map, down here. Last spring I ran out of grub, so I got some here. They've got a huge storage area in the kitchen and the place doesn't appear to be used in winter. I paid for the stuff of course. Left a note saying I was a trapper passing through and got caught short of supplies."

"It looks a long way off," I said.

"It's two full days' travel in good weather. Now here's my plan. If we're lucky, nobody will be around. There might be, since this is duck season, but we'll have to hope. I will grab my food and once I'm on my way, you can follow the road out of the camp to a main road and sooner or later you'll get a lift. It's the only sensible way I can think of to get you out."

So, there we were, headed out on a big caper at the end of which Mary and I would separate, forever.

We cached the canoe at the south end of the lake in a stand of balsam and I shouldered the big pack. It was light, containing only dried food, bedrolls, rainwear and another empty canoe pack for the food. Mary planned to fill both packs, hide one about a mile from the camp and return for it.

We made good time. The leaves being down, the bush was fairly open. We traveled over every kind of terrain you could imagine. A couple of hours from our lake we began to run into a series of high, sharp ridges—like fingers splayed across the landscape. They were dark, gray granite, patched with small stands of sumac and scrub oak. It was tough country to travel because between the fingers were swamps and beaver dams and the fingers themselves rose almost vertically in places. I felt like a mountain climber. Occasionally we walked along the edge of cliffs three stories high.

We spent the night on top of one of those ridges, tired as hell, under a clear sky dusted with stars.

Next morning was cold and clear. A couple of hours got us into gentler landscape—rolling hills of hardwoods with a few creeks to cross. The only thing that slowed us down was the occasional patch of swampy ground that we had to skirt. There was still absolutely no sign of humans. I felt like a *coureur de bois.*

Just about dusk we began to approach the lake. The land began to descend and we ran into softwoods, evergreens and birch.

Mary stopped just before we broke free of the trees. She pointed across the kidney-shaped lake. And there on the far shore, on a small promontory of maybe two acres was a group of long buildings huddled in the trees.

Smoke was coming from one of the chimneys.

Crabbe's Journal: 16

"Damn," said Mary in her disappointment. "This is going to complicate things."

We retreated into the trees again and flopped down in a copse of spruce, weary from the forced march. Over a snack of dry, crumbly bannock, Mary explained the layout of the hunt camp, drawing a map in the dirt with a stick. There were four buildings: a kitchen/dining-room cabin that could handle maybe twenty people; a rec hall with games tables and a big stone fireplace ("You know," she added, "like you see in all the ski ads."); and two small bunk cabins. The log buildings were bunched on the tip of the peninsula. A big dock of logs and planks stuck out into the lake.

The kitchen building was our objective. The owners stored food in there all year 'round—staples mostly. No perishable stuff, of course, but that wasn't what Mary wanted anyway. She planned to use the same routine she used last time, leaving money and a note in block letters printed, supposedly, by an old trapper.

As we lay there resting, waiting for darkness to complete its rise, I began to get nervous. The atmosphere was perfect for the jitters. The breeze had brought cloud cover with it and the sky held no light for us. A chilly ground fog rolled in off the lake. And old Crabbe, never brave at the best of times, got second thoughts. And when we began to hear voices floating across the lake and out of the mist, I got nervous as hell.

Somebody over in the rec hall was having a great time. Jagged bursts of laughter cut through the fog and as far as we could tell, every window in the building blazed with light. As time passed the noise seemed to increase, the laughter and shouting to burst out more often.

I suggested that we forget our plan and head back. I didn't like the sound of those voices. But Mary insisted that we at least take a crack at it.

"The weather is on our side," she said. "No one will see us if we're careful."

So a couple of hours after dark we moved out. If you ever want to experience real frustration, try walking through the bush on a completely starless night—silently. An eternity passed before we skirted the bay and moved onto the peninsula.

The buildings faced a compound about twice the size of a school gym. We drifted silently between the kitchen and one of the bunk houses, directly across from the rec hall. Crouching in the dark patch between the two log buildings, we cased the noisy and brightly lit hall. Nobody came or went.

"Maybe we should try for a peek in the back window," Mary whispered.

"Do we have to?" I tried to keep the shakes out of my voice but it didn't work.

"Yes, I think so. Let's go."

Before I could argue, Mary turned and, still in a crouch, scuttled to the rear of the bunk house. What could I do? I followed her. It was a small building, maybe six yards long and four along to the back where we stood up.

"Follow me," Mary whispered, and off she went into the black wall of trees.

A few minutes later we were behind the rec hall, hunkered down on the damp, needle-carpeted ground, up against the rough, peeled logs. There was only one small window in this wall, just above my head. From the raucous noises inside we figured two things: they were men, and they were drunk.

There were four of them, dressed very outdoorsy, like those dummies in the sports section of a big department store. Except these were mean-looking beggars. None had shaved for a few days and each was juiced to the eyeballs— you could tell from the way they moved with careful clumsiness as they played cards at a deal table before the blazing fire. One of them, the only one not overweight, damn near fell into the fireplace when he got up to poke the logs. Occasionally one would slam his cards onto the table with a roar, sending poker chips dancing all over the table and onto the dirty hardwood floor. The others would explode in braying laughter or shout what were probably curses— I couldn't quite tell. The portion of the room that I could see through that bathroom window was littered with beer and liquor bottles (I was too scared to be envious), boots, and a few cigarette packages.

In spite of my uneasiness I thought, what a bunch of jerks. Why come all the way up to a hunt camp in the middle of nowhere to get gunned up and play poker? Next morning they'd probably be barfing all over the landscape afraid to shoot a gun off for fear of cracking their aching skulls. Then after a couple of days of this stupidity they'd pile back into the city, bragging about their macho exploits and the quiet beauties of nature.

I got down off the splitting stump I'd been standing on and reported to Mary. She seemed pleased. In a few minutes we were back at the cook shack trying to jimmy the lock on the back door.

No sweat. We stepped into the dark store-room and shut the door behind us—slowly—because the hinges creaked. Mary fished a candle stub out of her shirt pocket, placed it on the floor and lit it, shielding the match with her hand. The candle threw a weak, watery light in a small pool, giving just enough illumination for us to work.

We located a fifty-pound sack of flour and hiked it into one of the canoe packs.

"Listen" Mary whispered, "I know where most of the stuff is kept so I'll bring it to you and you pack it."

"Gotcha," I replied with phoney enthusiasm. I wished we were out of there.

But on we worked, two little mice, sneaking food from the kitchen. I packed sugar, salt and six one-pound packages of loose tea. The first pack was full and I strapped it closed.

"Mary," I whispered into the darkness.

"What's the matter?" she sounded rattled too, now that I came to think about it.

"I'll take this one out and hide it in the trees," I said.

"Oh, yes. All right."

Easier said than done. That bloody pack was almost as heavy and awkward as mine were at the beginning of my trip. But I wrestled it outside and across the little yard behind the cabin and into the trees. For a moment I dreaded our walk back to our home, carrying the heavy packs. Then I remembered. I wasn't going back.

I stood there, just inside the trees, staring through the clammy fog into nothing. It's funny, but that's when it hit me. I wasn't going to see her again—ever. I'd promised I wouldn't try to contact her or break her secret. I'd sworn an oath—very formally too, with my hand on my chest and the whole bit.

Now I felt empty, yet at the same time full of sadness and loneliness. What the hell would I do without Mary? I began to cry, standing there in the black bush with the idiotic rumbling of the card-players in the background. I wanted to stay with her more than anything I had ever wanted in my life. But it just wasn't going to work out that way.

Well, there it is, I thought. Why stand around, wishing it was otherwise? It's decided. So get your ass in gear; get moving, don't think about it. Just do what has to be done.

Back I went, having wiped my face on my sleeve. A pile of dry goods was waiting for me and I began filling the second pack. Mary was waist-deep into one of the cupboards across the room.

"Eureka!" she said in an excited whisper.

"What? What's the matter?"

She had emerged from the cupboard and crawled into the tiny pool of light to show me four large tobacco tins.

"Oh, great," I said without much feeling. Although I was almost finished the tobacco Mary had brought with her to the bush, smoking was the farthest thing from my mind. It was just like her to think of something like that right in the middle of what I thought was a dangerous caper.

A shout from across the compound saved me from having to say anything else. I went rigid, instantly. Mary spun on the balls of her feet and scuttled over to blow out the candle. We kept still, straining to hear. A quick hiss told me she had wet the candle wick with her fingers.

There were two voices now. They were talking, half hollering. But the harsh voices came no nearer.

Without really thinking I said, "Stay here. I'm going to take a look."

Before she could answer, I crawled to the back door, opened it slowly to prevent squeaks, and slipped out, leaving it ajar. I ran silently across the wet ground to the corner of the bunk house and stopped to take a look. Nothing. Nothing but noises. In a crouch, I stole along the side wall, brushing the logs lightly. I was almost to the front door before I could get a full view of the rec hall.

They were still trying to light up the countryside. Two of them, the skinny one and the short, pudgy one, were standing on the deck that ran the full width of the building, leaning on the railing. I could hear only part of their conversation, just enough to pick up a lot of obscenities—another requirement, I've noticed, when men get together to rough it—and a few snatches of sentences. The skinny one had a laugh like a mule with one of its ears caught in the barn door. Pudgy guffawed with a deep, harsh laugh.

They both stood up and a few seconds later I heard water striking the ground, like a leak in an eavestrough. Skinny brayed. Then another stream of water could be heard. They were pissing off the deck, six feet or so to the ground.

"Ha, ha! Mine's farther. I win!" Pudgy shouted triumphantly. He followed this delicate statement with another guffaw.

Skinny kept silent. He turned slowly toward his companion. *Then* he laughed hysterically.

"You son of a bitch!" yelled the fat one. "Godammit, I'm soaked!" Then he stepped into Skinny and drove his fist into Skinny's throat with a vicious uppercut.

So much for friendship in the great outdoors. The two companions crashed onto the deck in a heap of clumsily flailing arms and legs. Their loud curses echoed all over the courtyard. A minute or so later the two other drunks stumbled out the door and in a chorus of shouts, curses and bursts of laughter, broke up the fight.

Just as things began to calm down, a big, dark German shepherd ambled through the doorway. I turned stone cold. "My God," I heard myself say. Where had this damn dog been when I checked out the rec hall through the window? How did I miss him?

Every molecule in my body focussed on that animal. If it smelled a stranger, we were done for.

As soon as it came onto the deck, the shepherd began to growl and snap and bark at the scuffling men. When the men quieted down, so did the dog, but not before one of the drunks yelled, "Shut up!" and cuffed it a few times.

After about five minutes (I think I held my breath for that long) the four friendly outdoorsmen began to go back in. I crossed a few fingers and toes, and I heard myself whispering, "That's it. Take the dog in with you. Go on, take him in."

As if obeying me, the fighters went through the screen door, letting it slap behind them. So far, so good. The other two spoke a few sentences, laughed. Then one of them went in. Slap, went the door again.

Three down, one to go. I was rigid with tension.

I groaned inwardly when I heard water again. Then it stopped. The guy must have had a bladder the size of a cow's udder. He was a big man, broad shouldered and heavy around the middle. He turned, finally, to the door and opened it.

But the dog didn't move. It stood still, dead still. With its nose up, it turned toward the cook house. I was sure I could hear it sniffing from where I was nailed to the ground in the shadow of the bunk house.

The man yelled over his shoulder "Get in here, dammit." But the shepherd was on the move, along the deck and down the steps in a flash. Then it stopped. Up went the nose. I prayed that the stink of their urine would screw up the dog's scenting apparatus.

But it trotted to the center of the compound and stopped again.

By this time the owner knew the mutt was onto something. He was drunk, but not that drunk. He came down the stairs, hand on the railing for balance, silently because he had no boots on.

"'Samatter, boy, smell a bear or somethin'?" he said excitedly.

I thought I couldn't be more scared—until I saw the pistol in his hand. What the hell was he doing with a handgun? I wondered. Even I knew they were illegal. He stalked across the compound after that damned dog, which had now begun to cast about with its nose to the ground.

Over in the cook shack Mary must have moved—I know I didn't—because that animal stopped dead, snapped its head up high, perked its ears and stood frozen for a second. Then it took off at a run straight as a spear toward the log cabin where Mary was trapped, alone. The owner stumbled along after.

And I did nothing. I was numbed with indecision, in shock. Every horrible sound that stabbed my ears—growling, the slam of a door, a scream, shouting—was another nail that fixed me to the spot.

The other three drunks piled out onto the deck in time to see the dog man shoving Mary across the compound at gunpoint. The mutt was jumping around her snarling and snapping at her heels and the hem of her shirttail. Mary stopped suddenly and caught the dog on the head with a quick, sharp kick and sent it yelping.

"Bitch!" the dog man shouted as he brought the gun through a clumsy arc and slammed it into the back of her head, at the same time shoving her forward. She pitched onto her face and the dog attacked again, going for the back of her neck.

By this time the other three were down the stairs trying to out-yell each other. The dog man pulled Mary to her feet and kicked the dog himself to keep it away.

"Lookit here, youse guys," he announced. "Caught this bitch in the store room, stealin' food."

I could hear them plainly now, practically smell their boozy breath.

"Well, well, well," said Skinny. "Best lookin' thief I ever saw." His voice was slurred, high-pitched like a finger on a chalkboard. He brayed.

The other two were too juiced up to really know what was going on. They kept asking the same stupid questions over and over, and when the whole bunch of them went into the hall, pushing Mary ahead of them, they barely made it up the stairs.

The last slap of the screen door snapped me out of my trance. The first thing I did was start to shake. The second thing was to sit down, lean my back against the cabin, and force my brain to work.

I turned and stared at the rec hall. I had to do something fast. I didn't even *want* to think of Mary in there with four drunks, and cruel ones at that. But: do what? I couldn't barge in there and fight four of them plus a huge, vicious dog. I'd never get her out that way.

No thoughts came. I stood, my hands clenched at my sides. I felt powerless.

Until I saw a burst of sparks erupt from the chimney. Then a whole bunch of puzzle pieces fell into place.

But I had to act fast. I ran behind the bunk house, across to the cook shack and into the dark bush behind it. Selecting a fat, tall birch right near where I'd left the pack, I yanked my knife out of the sheath and, holding it with both hands, cut a long vertical slit into the bark. Around the base and at head height I girdled the tree with two more slits. Forcing the blade into the vertical slit, I lifted the bark all down the cut. I resheathed the knife and, taking the raised edge of the bark in both hands walked around the tree, peeling off the cylinder of bark as I went. It sprung free easily.

I zipped into the cook shack, which the dog man had left open. Once inside I peeled strip after strip of birch bark, forming a big, loose pile just inside one of the cupboards along the side wall. For good measure I flashed back outside and scooped up a big handful of pine needles from under the shack. They were light and dry. I put them at the base of my pyramid of bark.

Next, I opened the huge, walk-in refrigerator, hoping the four outdoorsmen were as greedy as they were alcoholic. Sure enough, I found about a ton of steaks and ground beef. I ripped open the cellophane wrapping of the ground beef and stuffed as much as I could into my pants pockets. I grabbed three or four of the steaks and stepped outside the fridge, leaving the door open to give me light.

Still moving fast, I rummaged around in the half-filled pack and found the one-pound box of black pepper I had put there earlier. This I stuck inside my shirt.

The bark and needles caught fire immediately when I set a match to them. New birch bark gives off a fearsome crackling, black, smoky flame. Outside I darted, pausing to drop one of the steaks at the door. Another I lobbed right in front of the cook shack as I ran by; the third in the middle of the compound. I hoped they'd keep the dog busy, or at least distract him. The hamburger meat was insurance.

I ducked under the deck. The top of my head grazed the damp planks. There was lots of light still spilling from the windows but I was in shadow. While I waited I selected a heavy but easy to handle piece of hardwood from the woodpile under the deck.

The cook shack didn't take too long to be noticeable. Within five minutes the whole side wall was aflame. Great, wicked-looking yellow-orange flames lapped up the long wall, encouraged by the breeze.

Shouts. Pounding feet. Furious barking from inside. Slap of the screen door. Two men, Skinny and the dog man, tumbled down the steps and ran across the compound.

But just two. Dammit!

No time to wait. I bounded up the stairs, club in hand, reaching into jeans for a handful of meat. I threw open the door.

There were two large couches in the rec hall, one on each side of the big stone fireplace, and each held a sprawled, snoring drunk. The crack of doom wouldn't wake those guys, I thought. The card table between them had been knocked over, spilling poker chips, ash trays, glasses and bottles over the round carpet and hardwood floor. The place stank of sweat, smoke, dog and stale beer.

I crossed this main room in a second, tense, expecting the shepherd to attack. But it had been shut into one of the rooms off the main hall. I could hear it in there, going nuts, barking, whining and scratching. I dropped the meat.

"Mary! Mary!" I called in a low voice.

"In here! In here! Oh, thank God!" came a muffled voice from down the hall.

I crashed open the door to find her lying on the bed, hands tied behind her back. Her bush shirt had been ripped open down to her elbows and her T-shirt yanked up to expose her breasts. When I saw her I hoped the bastards would die in the fire.

I rolled her over, cut the ropes, picked up her coat from the floor and led her out of there. As we shot down the stairs I took a look at the fire. The two idiots were running back and forth, hollering at each other. They hadn't caught on yet, but they soon would.

Mary and I ran around the rec hall and dove into the trees as a great, earth-pounding slam of thunder cracked the sky open over the lake. Lightning lit up the compound.

It wasn't more than a few minutes before we circled the camp and got off that peninsula. I stopped at the shore.

"Still got your compass?" I said as she struggled into her jacket.

"I—I think so." she stammered. She was really rattled.

I took a bearing, hung the compass around my neck, got out the box of pepper. I sprinkled half of it in an arc at our feet.

"What's that for?" she asked.

"For the dog. Let's go."

I figured they might hunt us, if not that night, the next day. As long as that dog was in working order, we were in danger.

I checked the bearing again, grabbed Mary firmly by the wrist and struck off into a bush as black as the blackest coal.

What a night that was! After a while I calmed down and concentrated on leading Mary by compass back through the bush. And, I'll tell you, the compass was in control. A short but nasty cloudburst had soaked us and darkness and fog got together to reduce our visibility to a couple of yards. It was like being caught in a wet, black bag. Every once in a while I'd blunder into a spruce or the trunk of a maple. I was completely disoriented and that compass was my only link with reality.

Mary was acting very strangely. One minute she'd be panic-stricken and in a big hurry. The next, calm, as if she'd forgotten what happened to her. Her face had a wasted look when we had left the rec hall. I was glad I couldn't see it now.

On and on we trudged in an impossible attempt to go quickly; tripping, slapped by dripping branches, tired, wet, very cold. I never let go of her except when I fell, or she did.

After a lifetime, the soggy air around us gradually changed color, from black to slowly lightening shades of gray. We kept moving and the terrain began to get rougher.

Although it had got lighter, the fog was still thick and the bush was ghostly gray, with the darker shapes of trees looming around us. It was impossible to find landmarks. I recognized nothing.

I was cheered up a little, though, when we met a creek, probably the same one we'd waded the day before.

"Mary, what do you think? Do you recognize this stream?"

"I—I guess so," she answered weakly. She wasn't even looking at the water when she said that.

I looked at her. The only sound was the purling of water over rocks and under logs. She was out of it, that was certain. I'd have to get us all the way back on my own.

Okay, I thought. No choice. So, do it.

I asked her if she was warm enough. It seemed to be getting colder as we breathed clouds that were absorbed into the fog. I got no answer from her. So I took out the pepper box, led Mary into the creek up to our knees, turned and dumped the rest of the pepper along the shore where we'd entered. Dropping the box in the water, I led Mary downstream for a hundred yards or so. When we left the stream I took a new bearing and led her into the eerie fog.

Over the next few hours a strong wind built up. The gusts tossed the naked branches of the hardwoods and drove away the heavy mist. I estimated it was around noon when the rain came back. By the time we entered the ridge country I knew two things.

First, we were on course. Mary's compass had kept us on track.

Second, we were in deep trouble. The wind was bitter cold, with a nasty edge to it. The rain pelted us like bullets shot out of the gusts. Our clothes were wet through and we were in danger of hypothermia. To stop moving might mean allowing those maniacs to catch up with us. There was no telling how they would take revenge. If they were smart they'd stay in on a day like this. If the pepper worked the dog would be useless to them.

If. Lots of Ifs. Not sure what to do, I pushed on, deep into the rough country, climbing the first of the steep granite ridges. Once up on top I tried to catch sight of the pursuers but in that weather there was little visibility. I heard nothing but the howling wail of the wind, saw nothing through sheets of rain but gray sky, gray trees, gray rock.

Coming down off that first ridge was wicked. I don't know if you've ever tried rock climbing. Going up is not too hard. Coming down is. You're actually *backing* down, searching for hand- and foot-holds under and behind you. Doing it on rain-slicked granite is worse.

So once we were down safely and into a steep gulley tangled with fallen trees and scrub I took stock again. I decided to stop for the night. If we could get a fire going against the rock, out of the wind, we might be able to huddle together and keep warm, maybe even dry our clothes.

Who was going to chase us in this weather anyway? I thought. It'd be crazy. Those jerks were probably too hung over to move, let alone push through the bush in the black of night. And the flaming cook house should have kept them busy for a long time.

So I put the plan to Mary. Her eyes grew large with fright.

"No, no, no. Got to keep moving," she groaned. She was barely making sense; just kept chanting, "No, can't stop, can't stop, no."

What could I do? She was not sensible. She tried to head off on her own when I insisted we had to rest and dry out.

I should have tied her up. I should have done something to force her to stop. But I didn't.

Crabbe's Journal: 17

The wind had dropped and steadied by dark and the rain drizzled coldly. We scrambled and scratched over the rugged terrain, climbing and slipping. Mary began to make some sense and I began to hope that if we made it through the night we'd be okay.

One particular ridge would make a mountain goat worry, but we started up, compelled to push on. It went up steeply for maybe two stories. There were lots of hand- and foot-holds all right—on a sunny day it would be a fun climb. But with numb, cold fingers and feet like frozen clubs, with twenty-four hours of travel behind you and a body half-dead, it was tough. We tore the flesh on our fingers and banged our knees a million times. The tedious hiss of rain on the rocks was broken by exhausted grunts of exertion.

Up we toiled, so slowly, unable to see the top until we were almost there. I got over the top first and turned to drag Mary the last few feet. We lay there, breathing heavily.

Finally I sat up.

"We made it, Mary," I said. "That's the toughest climb finished. I remember. There's only a couple of ridges left—

easy ones—so we're home free. Just a few hours from the lake. We'll never be chased this far."

"Let's rest," was all she said. But I took that as a good sign. She was over her panic. And she was back in touch with herself, enough to know she was tired out.

Turning our backs to the black pit we'd just climbed out of, we picked our way among the rocks and into a small stand of scrub oaks.

"I'm going to make a fire," I said. "We'll feel better if we can warm up a bit. You sit down." I took Mary by the shoulders and pushed her onto a rock under one of the oaks.

Ten minutes later I coaxed a tiny, smoky orange flame from shreds of birch bark and fairly dry twigs. Once the fire had caught on I stood and said, "I'll go hunt up some more wood."

"I'll help," she said, rising unsteadily.

"No, no. You stay here. I can manage."

"No, I could use the exercise," she said and laughed weakly.

I was so happy and relieved to hear that laugh that I didn't argue with her, just turned and walked a few yards into the black curtain of the bush and groped around in the dark for wood. When I came back a few minutes later the little fire was smoking and dying out so I had to work on it to nurse it back to the point where it would accept bigger sticks. I could hear only the snap of burning twigs, the hiss of rain on wet ground and rock and on the branches that gave only a little protection. The fire looked almost homey. I could feel a little warmth from it and began to think we'd really made it. We had survived. We would go back, get dry clothes, build the biggest damned bonfire ever, and crawl into our toasty, down sleeping bags. And sleep for days.

But I guess it doesn't work that way.

After a few minutes I grew concerned that I couldn't hear her. I called her name. No answer. Then again. I retraced our steps. I fretted and ran around, growing more and more frantic. The brave little fire was forgotten and soon died. Around me were only the dark of the woods and the hiss of the rain.

I suppose all along I knew what had happened. After a while I stopped looking and calling. And when the cold dawn leaked enough thin gray light into the landscape I set my jaw and forced myself to look over the edge of the steep rock we had worked so hard to conquer.

Mary was down there.

She lay on her back, twisted and broken by her fall to the jagged rocks on the valley floor.

I don't want to spend a lot of time on this next part. I did what I had to do and that's all there is to say about it.

The strange thing was, at that time I didn't—couldn't—cry. Numb and mechanical and calm, I was as empty of emotion as she was of life. I seemed to have complete presence of mind and, after a long time staring at her and building up the courage to climb down and do what was necessary, I carefully picked my way to the bottom.

I couldn't take her back to civilization, that was obvious. And I couldn't bury her in the rocky ground. Not even a rock grave would keep animals away for long.

I spent all day gathering wood, carefully avoiding looking at her as I returned with each armload. The constant activity kept me warm and, since there was no rain, my clothing dried out a little. Dusk had arrived by the time I finished. The light breeze that blew all day had removed the clouds and dried the air. The first stars began to show when I lit the fire, using several starter fires with lots of birch bark and branches with the soggy bark stripped off.

As the last light faded I watched from the top of the ridge until I was certain the raging fire would not quit on me. By then it was dark. The stars would give me enough light to travel by if I moved slowly. I took a bearing with the compass, said "Goodbye, Mary," to the flames that crackled and raged, and turned and left the place. The roar of the inferno gradually faded behind me, and the leaping shadows seemed to show me the way to go.

Crabbe's Journal: 18

The long walk to the lake was uneventful. It's a little creepy, traveling alone in the bush at night, surrounded by varying shades of blackness. The night sounds are spooky and your own noises, even in a wet forest, seem loud. But I was too bone-tired, damp, and cold to think about it. Besides, the last—what?—forty-eight hours had wrung all my emotions out of me. I just obeyed the compass, ignoring everything else.

When I reached the lake, I found the canoe easily. Soon I was back at the campsite. It seemed strange not to be greeted with a loud hello or a laugh as I pulled the boat out of the water and hid it out of habit in the usual place.

I'm ashamed to say, though, that I did not miss Mary. Though deserted and forlorn, that campsite meant only one thing to me then. I got a fire going quickly and soon had my damp clothing hung on sticks around it at a safe distance. Once in the tent, I stuffed one sleeping bag inside another and climbed inside. The warmth was unbelievable, flooding around me, dragging me to sleep.

I slept for at least two days, rising only to drink water

and relieve myself. When I finally did emerge, dressed in the extra clothing that Mary always kept stored in the tent, it was mid-day, sunny and cold.

The first thing I thought of was food. There wasn't much around the campsite—after all, that's why we went on the raid in the first place—but I managed some strong Labrador tea and dried fish. I ate till I couldn't pack away another molecule and, out of habit, took my last cup of tea down to the lake. Then I hit the sack again.

I guess my system was back on schedule because I awoke at dawn. After making up the fire, I made a trip to the bush and recovered one of Mary's food caches. She had taken a variety of food—smoked fish, jerky, berries, tubers and stuff—and packed it all into a bundle that would last her a month. After wrapping the bundle in plastic to water-proof it, she'd hang it in a tree at the edge of the campsite. I had helped her all summer and there were nine or ten of them around.

After breakfast I threw some pieces of fat, some jerky and a chopped up lily root into a little water in a pot and put the pot on a low fire. The stew would be for supper.

I sat there for a while, tending the fire, adding sticks until the water boiled, then banking the fire so as to give a steady, simmering heat.

And, do you know, I waited for them, but the tears wouldn't come. I *tried* to cry, thought of all the good times we'd had, the things we'd done together but nothing would come. There I was, dressed in her clothing, everything I was doing the result of her teaching, the fact that I was alive at all due to her courage, and I couldn't even cry for her. Dry eyes were my thanks. I was disgusted with myself.

But then that was a stupid notion. I loved her. In fact, at that moment I felt that she was the only person I ever *had* loved. Maybe tears didn't prove anything.

I began to think about Mary rather than the fact that she was dead. What did I know of her? Almost nothing. And yet everything I needed to know. Her approximate age. Her physical appearance. The play of many emotions across her strong, beautiful features. A little bit about her personality: she was the only female I knew who was a *person* to me.

Soon, as I thought about her, I remembered the canvas canoe pack she kept hidden in the bush. Would it give me answers to the million questions I asked myself every day? What was in her past? What was a beautiful, intelligent woman doing hiding in the bush for over a year? Who was she?

My curiosity soared again. I *had* to see that pack's contents. I didn't feel I'd be betraying her. There was no need for secrecy now.

And that, strangely, was what did it. As soon as I thought that thought—that the campsite could be discovered now and it didn't matter—the tears came. And soon I was on my knees in the dirt, hunched over by the cheery little fire, wracked by deep, tearing sobs that came from way down inside me. When they say your heart breaks I know what they mean. Something had been torn away, leaving empty pain.

The sun was directly overhead in a cold sky by the time I found the pack under a big spruce tree that had a skirt so low it brushed the ground. The hiding place was pretty close to the campsite as I figured it would be. Having lugged the pack to the fireside, I left it alone while I checked the stew and made some tea. I filled the pipe and smoked for a bit.

Then I opened the pack, crying a little as I did so.

Over the next couple of days I pieced together what I could about Mary's life before her escape. I had to use a lot of detective work on the letters, pictures, magazine and newspaper articles, documents and other stuff I found. There were many false starts too.

I want to tell this so it makes sense rather than just write down an inventory of the contents.

Mary was a university professor. She went to the University of Toronto, McMaster and Harvard, where she got a Doctor of Philosophy degree in History. Then she became an assistant prof at Laurentian University. I read the published articles in the pack and I gather she was a left-winger and an environmentalist. She seemed to think society was sick ("out of touch with itself" was a phrase in one article). Society was like a living creature that had picked up an illness, so the organism had to throw lots of its resources into fighting the illness, and that threw the whole organism out of whack until either the organism died or the illness died. I didn't understand the whole essay. There was lots of stuff in it about misusing the environment and wasting resources and so on. She didn't say everything was wrong—I don't mean that—but the wrong things had importance and the wrong people had control.

There were quite a few articles on historical questions too. Pretty boring stuff. But she was one smart woman, I'll tell you.

But she wasn't *cold* smart. I've met a lot of smart people at different times and most of them seemed stand-off-ish, unemotional, as if when their brains grew they pushed all the feelings out of the way. And most of them seemed to think that *showing* feeling was some kind of weakness. Most of the smart people my father dragged home were boring snobs. He wanted me to be like that.

Mary wasn't like that at all. She always seemed to know what I was feeling, and she cared about that. Oh, she didn't treat me like glass or anything like that. Hell, sometimes she told me off and didn't hold back. But she could do that because I knew she cared about *me,* not my clothes or my money, not my high marks at school or my father's job or where I lived—*me.* I never met anyone who made me feel *necessary.* Not important: necessary. I mattered to her.

What I mean is, Mary was a tremendously wise, smart woman who didn't come across like a dried up old intellectual.

Anyhow, to continue. Mary was married. I found some pictures of her husband: just an ordinary looking guy with a thin face and black hair and big, sad dark eyes. He worked at the same university doing research in Physics. She had a whole stack of his degrees too, along with a bunch of articles I couldn't understand. But there was one little book he wrote, "No Nukes is Good Nukes," which was a humorous attack on nuclear arms and had some serious questions about nuclear power stations. I guess he and Mary were activists. There were some buttons in the pack with slogans on them—anti-nuclear.

As I said, I pieced all this together over a couple of days, days that were hard on my emotions, full of crying fits and depression.

But one thing still threw me. I knew lots more about her, but I still didn't know what the hell she was doing out in the middle of nowhere. Now the mystery was even greater. Why leave all that behind?

I went back through all the stuff, rereading everything more carefully—I had just skimmed it before. Gradually, the background was filled in. It was while I was flipping through a copy of a university quarterly that I found something new. A couple of newspaper clippings fell out from between the pages. I opened them up, realizing that I hadn't seen them the first time around.

PHYSICS PROFESSOR
INJURED IN DEMONSTRATION

The report said that Mary's husband, who was taking part in an anti-nuclear demonstration at the provincial government buildings, had been jostled from the crowded sidewalk into the path of a taxi. He had been seriously injured and rushed to a hospital.

The other article was written a couple of days later. It gave a follow-up on the march and mentioned in passing that the injured professor was on the critical list and doctors were afraid he would die. If he lived, he would be totally par-alyzed and mentally deficient, since the injuries were to his head and spine. He was on life-support machines. The report ended with an opinion that if people would only stay home instead of taking part in "radical" protests, that sort of thing wouldn't happen.

Well, I knew where he was, anyway. He must have died. I mean, a person like Mary certainly wouldn't *leave* him in the hospital, plugged into the machines, and run off into the bush. Their old letters made it clear that they loved each other very much. (And, I'm ashamed to admit, I felt a little jealous about that.)

But all that *still* didn't get me much farther ahead, did it? If he had died, why run away? She wasn't on any holi-day, that was for sure; she was *hiding*. It didn't seem possi-ble that she was a crook or a spy.

Finally, I gave up, totally frustrated. I'd invested a few rainy, cold, dreary autumn days in getting to know her past. I couldn't see that I would find out anything more.

Methodically, because I knew she would want me to, I burned everything except the pack in my morning fire. It was a strange feeling. I was pretty upset, crying and sniff-ing all through, feeding the mementoes of two lives into the flames. Two important lives. Two decent people who loved each other, and certainly others, and were good at spreading their love around. He must have been like that. They lived their lives looking beyond themselves.

Which is more than I've ever done. Now they were dead. Life isn't fair. It isn't even logical.

That was one of her favorite expressions, I thought as I tore her letters into shreds and gave them to the fire. "Life isn't fair, Crabbe," she'd say whenever I was in the middle of one of my complaining fits. She wouldn't say it sarcastically, just stated it like it was a thought that had just occurred to her. The first time it came out was just a couple of weeks after I had come to her. I was going hell bent in a tirade against my phoney parents and stupid teachers and boring life—all that crap. We had been swimming and were sitting on a huge granite slab that rose out of the water near our campsite, letting the hot sun dry us.

When I stopped for breath, she said, "Look, Grumpy, you've got a family, a house to live in, a place to make your mind and body grow, money to do some interesting things, parents who care about you—in spite of what you say. What the hell do you want, jam on it?"

I laughed, without wanting to. I had a great aunt who used that old expression as often as she could.

"No, don't laugh, Kiddo," she said seriously, getting wound up like she always did when she was trying to make a point. "Look, whose life *is* it, anyway?"

"Mine."

"Okay. If it's not a life you like, who should fix it?"

I was trapped. I had been running through my "blame list" as I often did when I was depressed or unhappy (which, then, was most of the time).

"I guess I should," I said. "But—"

"Never mind, 'guess,'" she interrupted. "It's a fact Crabbe. Waiting around for somebody to change your life for you is a loser's game. Who's going to do it? You're not a child, remember. And if some fairy godmother *did* offer to take on the job, how could she possibly get it right? Only *you* know what *you* want. She'd fail. And that'd just give you somebody else to blame."

She paused for a breath, then continued.

"You know what I think, Crabbe? I think a person reaches maturity when he strikes the last name off the blame list."

We talked some more about all that. The sun on our skin and the beauty of the day made it hard to be ambitious. Then she said it.

"Well, life isn't fair, Crabbe. But trying to build a life of *significance* despite the unfairness can be exciting. I don't mean soft or easy or contented. I mean exciting. Philosophers might give that attitude a fancy title, like existentialism. A life without fairness is always worth living; a life without significance isn't."

"Who decides what is significant?" I asked.

"Whose life is it?"

All this I remembered as I sat by the fire on that somber day, feeding the last shreds of paper to the flames.

Then, WHAM!—it hit me.

She had killed her husband!

As soon as the thought hit me, I was certain of it.

I don't know what you think of mercy killing. I don't know what I think of it either. But a lot of people are against it, and so is the law. Mary knew that.

She took her husband's life, and the rest of her own, into

her own hands. She committed murder, merciful murder, then ran away.

I pictured her visiting him, standing beside the bed with its starched, white linen, talking to the wasted man who had no idea of her presence. I saw her kiss him softly on his pale forehead, then do something to the machines that kept him in a world he should have been allowed to leave with dignity.

It was coming on dark by the time all this was figured out and all the possessions were burned. It was getting dark very early these days. Knowing the answers about her didn't make me feel any better. But it made me admire her more, knowing she had had the courage to do that.

God, how I wished she was with me!

Crabbe's Journal: 19

Remember what I said about omens? Well, sometimes omens are cold and hard and easy to figure. I had spent quite a few days moping around, feeling depressed and sorry for myself, not doing much of anything, when I woke one morning to find four inches of snow had fallen during the night. It was still coming down in fat, wet flakes undisturbed by wind. My firewood and equipment had disappeared under soft mounds of snow and the landscape looked suddenly and completely whitewashed.

So, I had a decision to make. Very soon I'd be trapped for the winter. My exit required open water and portages that had no more than a foot or so of snow: I couldn't imagine ploughing through any more than that with a canoe on my shoulders. Our little bay had a skin of ice on it every morning.

It was a matter of leaving now, before a real cold snap froze up the waterways completely, or staying all winter. An easy decision. But it took that snowfall to yank me out of the fog of depression I was in.

I spent the morning getting fed, checking what equipment I had, and carefully studying the map. Again, I had two choices: go back the way I came or try to work out a better route, one that was either easier or quicker.

I was going to try another route. The time I spent coming down river before I fell over the falls would be doubled or quadrupled going the other way. That current had been pretty strong. And there was still the other, narrow creek, after the first lake, the one I tried to learn to steer on. All that upriver travel and the many portages made me shudder.

So I studied the map for a long time. I could find Ithaca Camp easily enough and there were a few possible routes. But I had to try and figure out by the contours whether I would have to travel up or down a particular river, to keep my eye open for rapids and falls, to estimate the length of portages (the length changes with the seasons and so does the depth of rapids).

All that took some thought but I put together a route that was a bit longer than my original and, I hoped, a lot easier. It was late afternoon by then and the snow had stopped. A breeze began to bend the smoke from the fire. That would mean the stormclouds might move off during the night.

I searched out another of Mary's caches and lugged it back to the fire. It was then I realized that the deep snow was going to be a problem. My legs were damp from snow melting on my pants. And I knew now that in winter dampness or wetness was my greatest enemy. It's impossible to keep warm if you're wet. If you stay dry and stay on the move it can get supercold and you'll still be safe (up to a point of course). Your body heat will keep you warm.

So what I needed was leggings. Since I planned to carry only one pack, I took another and cut it up and, in the fading light, I made a crude pair of leggings that tied on just above my knees. Then, since I was such a wonderful tailor, I took another pack, cut three holes in it, and had a "coat" that would come in handy if I ran into cold wind or more snow.

It was just coming on light when I got up. The snow looked light gray, the line of the trees almost black. I was kind of looking forward to the trip after doing nothing for so long. I tried not to look too far forward, though, to my coming back to the city. I decided to take one day at a time.

I didn't bother with a fire—all the equipment was packed up—just drank some water (I kept a bottle in my sleeping bag each night so it wouldn't freeze) and munched a mouthful of the awful but nourishing stuff Mary kept in the caches—jerky, fat, and berries all pounded together into chewy bars. After a last-minute inventory (waterproofed sleeping bags, tent and fly, extra clothes, food, map and compass, matches—waterproofed this time!) I was standing on the shore, ready to go.

After the canoe was loaded up, I turned and tried to work up a goodbye to what had been my home for five months or more. But it looked so different, snow-covered and empty. From where I stood you could hardly even tell anyone had been there; it looked like just another clearing, cold and desolate.

So I turned, shook the snow off my boots, and pushed off out onto the lake.

There's a strange beauty to the bush in winter. It was still overcast that morning and the landscape was a blend of black, white and shades of gray. The lake was the color of shale, and smooth. With its brightness muted without the sun the snow was a softened white, stretching away from the water. There were patches of birch along the shore. The black blotches on the white bark and the dark, smaller branches brought them out of the background in sharp relief. The gray hardwoods stood naked and cold. In the distance the hills showed a faint touch of reddish brown. The only color in the scene came from the stands of vivid green spruce and cedars that crowded together in the low places.

I won't record all the details of the trip. The weather held pretty well; that's to say it was cold but not cold enough to lock up all the lakes. The shorelines were all fringed with ice, though. I got some light snow, some sun—a good mixture. And I made pretty good time, all in all. For one thing, I had only one pack to carry. That meant one trip on the portages because I could take both pack and canoe at one time. For another, I was in good shape, strong and able to work all day.

By the morning of the fourth day I was ready for the last leg. I had to do a portage of around eight miles and I'd end up on the shore of the lake Ithaca Camp was on. My plan was to spend the night where the portage began and devote the next day to the crossing. The map showed the terrain to be rolling hills—challenging but nothing terrible.

I got up at dawn as usual and hung the sleeping bags while I prepared a big breakfast with lots of strong tea and more food than usual. (The bags have to be hung so as to dry out the moisture that gathers in them during the night from your body heat and breathing. If you don't do that, the bag will be cold the next night and never really warm up.)

The wind should have been a warning. But I was anxious to attack that portage. As I cooked and ate breakfast, the wind was picking up speed quickly and turning colder. You should always pay attention to the wind if you live outdoors. Sailors know that. So did I, but, as I said, my mind was on other things. I had no idea I was about to walk into the teeth of the worst and earliest blizzard for years and almost kill myself in the process. I was at water level in hilly country. There's no real horizon in country like that and the wind is cut down and deflected by the hills.

Anyway, off I went, trudging through the snow in my classy leggings. I was following what was probably a fishermen's portage in summer so, aside from the difficulties of walking uphill in snow, the going was pretty reasonable.

Another thing I didn't notice early enough though was body temperature. Normally, a while after I started working, I'd be shedding some clothing so as not to get damp with sweat. But today I had no desire to remove anything. As a matter of fact, when I topped a hill later in the morning and put down the canoe and pack to rest, I felt colder and dug out my bag-coat to give me some protection against the rising wind.

It was bitter cold by now. My breathclouds were snatched away each time I exhaled. Around the edges of my toque and on my sideburns the water vapor from my breath had frozen to form a rim of ice.

I looked up at the top branches of the hardwoods to see them waving frantically. Lots of wind up there, I thought. There was no sun in the darkening sky, a sky of deep gray with a tinge of purple in the northwest. When the snow arrived, tiny flakes whipping frantically around, I knew I was in for something.

The problem was, I figured I must be halfway to the lake: it would be crazy to turn back. So I shouldered my burdens and marched on, weaving downhill through the trees, trying not to slide.

It wasn't long after that that I was wearing every piece of clothing I owned. I had one pair of wool socks stuffed down my neck to make a scarf and another on my hands. The snow was thick now and even in the little valleys between the hills it was swirling and driving, piling up quickly on the ground and packing into the creases in my clothing. I must have looked like a ghost. I wore the compass on a thong around my neck and consulted it frequently because I couldn't see very far. I was glad my head was under the canoe, protected from the angry wind.

Soon fear began to hammer away at me, strengthening with every gust of the icy wind. I felt that I had to keep moving so I wouldn't freeze. I knew I was still on course. But even when I reached the lake, what then? Try to cross it in a blinding blizzard?

I was between two high hills now in a gully where the wind was a bit less violent. I decided to rest. Flipping the canoe off my shoulders, I dropped the pack and sat down on it. No longer protected by the hull of the boat, my face and hands soon felt the sting of the wind and I feared that frostbite was on the way.

I looked around. Over on my right, about ten yards along the gully, was a huge deadfall. A thick maple had fallen from the steep bank, its roots ripped from the shallow soil, and had come to rest on a giant granite boulder. Between the boulder and the roots was a sort of cave.

When I saw that, I made a quick and, as it turned out, wise decision. Animals hole up in storms, I thought. So do people if they have any sense.

I lugged all my truck over to the spot. Using my paddle, I scooped most of the snow out of the "cave," there wasn't much because the big root network, clogged with dirt, took the force of the wind. I left enough snow to make a floor by packing it down. Then I dragged the canoe to the windward side and propped it between rock and tree. I pulled the tent out of the pack and, using the nearly horizontal tree trunk as a ridge pole, fashioned a roof by tying the lines to the bottom gunwale of the canoe on one side and weighing down the other side with rocks. I packed snow around the little house, banking it with the paddle, so that no wind could enter from the ground level.

I checked the thing over very carefully, walking around it a couple of times, then entered on the leeward side, dragging the pack in after me. The only problem now was that the snow floor would be cold. I took off my canvas packcoat, folded one of the sleeping bags and stuffed it inside, making a thick pillow. I sat down on it and leaned against the tree roots, grateful for the chance to rest. The tiny cave soon warmed up.

I could still hear the wind howling and wailing now, which meant that the storm was getting even worse. The nylon roof of my cubbyhole rustled and snapped, reminding me that it would need support against the weight of snow. Quickly scooting outside, I felt my way along the maple trunk, punished by the wind and blinded by the snow. I got my paddle and snapped off a few branches from the tree trunk.

Back inside, I wedged the three branches between the boulder and the ground. On the canoe side I used the paddle as a rafter. Things looked pretty secure now. I was dry, warm and safe.

Naturally, I immediately thought of food and was soon gnawing away on jerky. Water was a bit of a problem. I ate snow very slowly so as not to cool myself down too much. Once my thirst was gone the warmth and rest made me drowsy. I soon dropped off.

I dozed on and off all night, coming fully awake after daylight had arrived. Of course the only way I knew it *was* daylight was to lift a corner of the nylon and push a lot of the snow aside. The wind was still about its work but seemed less severe. There was one hell of a lot of snow out there too.

The cave felt strange, sort of oppressive, and until I pulled the nylon aside a bit I found it hard to get my breath. That could only mean that my cave had been sealed off by the drifting snow and I had been rebreathing the air inside.

I didn't want to leave the flap open; icy air quickly sneaked in, bringing gusts of fine, powdered snow with it. So I snapped off a twig from the maple and carefully punched a half dozen holes through my roof in places where the nylon didn't quite meet the rock.

A bit of light came in, enough to let me grope around and find some food. I filled a cup with snow as an experiment to see if the cave's heat was enough to melt it. Nope, although it was pretty warm inside, enough so the nylon roof, which sagged between my makeshift rafters with the weight of the snow, was coated with a film of ice.

I sat back against the roots and munched some food. I started to think about what I would do when I got back. Don't think I missed my parents, or anybody else for that matter, because I didn't. But I really had no plan, or many choices.

Or did I? Maybe I had more choices than I thought. One thing I was sure about: *I* would decide. I'd had it with living my life the way other people wanted. Mary had told me, "Waiting around for somebody else to fix *your* life is a fool's game." Well, I was ready to take the responsibility. No more complaints about how hard done by I was. Hell, if I could make it out of this storm I could handle the rest of it.

That may not sound like much, but it was a start. And it gave me a good feeling.

In the bush, if you don't take responsibility for yourself you just don't last. You go home hating the place or you don't make it back at all. Sure, it's good if you have somebody like Mary there to help you and get you ready, but when it comes right down to it, you're on your own. That was the difference between her and my parents (and the other adults I'd known). Mary would teach me anything—cooking over a fire, where to find dry wood in a rainstorm, how not to get lost—but somehow she always made it clear that the reason she taught me was so I wouldn't need her around all the time. My parents were the opposite, always trying to make me dependent so they could control me. They picked my school, my career, even tried to choose my friends (then wondered why I never had any). Mary had said to me, "The greatest compliment you can give a teacher, Crabbe, is to say, 'I don't need you any more.'"

Well, I figured I was ready to begin to live my life. I was healthy, strong, reasonably smart, and young. The fact that I didn't have a clue what I'd *do* with my life didn't bother me at all. One step at a time.

Having thought that, I fell asleep again.

Crabbe's Journal: 20

I spent, altogether, two nights, one and a half days holed up, sleeping and thinking. When I finally came out I found myself in a different world. Around me the carved lines of great, swooping snowdrifts threw shadows across the snow, softening the bright morning light. Above, the sky was a hard, clear blue and the air was cold. The bush was so quiet I could hear my own breathing.

I suppose an artist would have been thrilled to death with the pattern of shadow and dazzling white, the brittle branches against the blue sky; but me, I just stood there calculating how I was going to handle this latest wrinkle in the saga of Crabbe the Traveller. Where I stood, right outside my nest (now shaped like an igloo) I was hip deep in snow and God only knew what was waiting for me farther on.

One thing was sure: I'd have to abandon the canoe.

But soon I was packed up again, slogging through the snow. It was hard going, I'll tell you. In the places where the wind had got up some momentum during the storm the snow was only knee deep, but I had to plough through drift after drift as I went along. Some, deeper than my hips, I had to go around. Progress was very slow.

By late afternoon the sky was jammed up with low, ugly-looking clouds that came in on a freshening wind, a wind that came head-on against me.

But I kept on, mostly out of frustration in spite of the fading light and the unwelcome snow that began to sting my face. I repeated to myself, "Where in the hell is that lake?" I figured the most I had to cover that day was three, maybe four miles, yet here I was, still slogging. Though I was certain I was on course, I checked the compass every few minutes and even hauled out the map to double-check.

Well, I *was* right. I reached the lake at nightfall. Completely exhausted, I leaned against the trunk of a thick maple as I looked out over the ice, for the lake had frozen during the blizzard for as far out as I could see. My legs felt rubbery and I panted from an attack on a hard-packed drift that swept up from the shore in a huge curve.

As my breath returned so did my common sense. I had reached the lake, but so what? I was still miles from nowhere and landbound.

In the rapidly fading light, back to the wind, eyes squint-ed against the swirling snow, I checked the map. Ithaca Camp was the only place near and it was a few miles northeast from where I was. Though probably closed for the winter, it would at least have shelter.

I quickly dug some food out of the pack, stuffing my mouth with jerky. As I chewed, I took a final check of my clothing.

This last leg was going to be rough. I would be traveling in the dark and no light would come from that snowy sky. The wind was stronger here, slamming against the trees, tossing the branches which snapped and clashed in protest. The waving trunks groaned and squeaked eerily.

I was wearing every article of clothing I owned, including the canvas pack-coat which was frozen stiff and crusted with ice and snow. My toque was yanked down across my brows and over my ears. My parka (inherited from Mary) was buttoned up tight but I snugged the drawstring on the hood a little more. Hood and toque were stiff, rimmed with frozen breath. My hands felt okay in the mitt-socks and my feet were only a little chilly. All systems go.

I set out into the teeth of the wind without the pack. I couldn't carry the thing another step. So this trip was all or nothing.

Why didn't I hole up again, as I should have? I'm not sure. Looking back, I think the reason was I felt so *close.* I was only a few miles from where I wanted to go and I kept thinking, just a little farther, just a couple of hours, and I'd be out of the cold. Which wasn't sensible at all, of course. A couple of miles in a blizzard is a long, long way.

I tried to stick to the shore of the lake because the land was fairly flat and most of the drifts, though packed harder here, were only knee deep or so. But Mommy Nature always makes you pay. Out of the bush meant into the wind, which raced freely across the lake like a steel-cold demon, snatching away my body heat as I stumbled along, eyes on either my compass or the few feet of snow in front of me. It was dark now. There was snow on the wind—not much, but driven horizontally until the wind struck the trees on the rising shoreline and dropped its burden.

I don't know how many times I fell before I lost my mitts; I fell forward in a deep drift and threw my arms out to break the fall. But the snow was deep and I went in up to my shoulders, burying my face. I cursed and struggled in frustration, unable to push my way out because my arms just kept plunging into the snow, nothing to push against. Finally I managed to roll sideways, only to find that my mitts were lost in the drift and impossible to find in the dark. Snow was jammed way up my sleeves and I had a hell of a time digging it out.

It wasn't long after that that my hands, which I tried to withdraw up the now snowy sleeves, developed a stinging sensation in them. The same sensation slowly invaded my feet. Then it went away. I thought with relief that I was beginning to warm up, since the pain was gone. Then a horrible thought struck me and I tried flexing my fingers. They were very stiff. Then the toes. Same thing. I realized with a shudder that they hadn't warmed up. The pain went away because the tissue was beginning to freeze.

I really got scared then and did something stupid. I began to run. But I didn't get very far before the run became a stagger and I fell again, gulping in big mouthfuls of the frosty air. I was feeling cold all over now and didn't rise. I didn't want to. I sat in the snow, drew my knees up to my stomach and tucked my chin into my collar.

Maybe I'll just sit and rest awhile, I thought. My breathing became more regular. Boy, was I tired. I needed a rest. I began to feel very comfortable. The cold was going away and I felt less afraid, and then not afraid at all—almost contented.

You know, some people say reading is a waste of time and maybe for them it is. But as I sat there watching tiny grains of snow dancing around in front of my face I thought, this is just like a story I read by Jack London. Something about a fire. The guy in the story froze to death but just before he drifted off he lay down in a snow drift hallucinating, waiting happily to fall asleep.

Well, I didn't think I wanted to go to sleep—at least not yet. But as soon as the image of that poor fool crossed my mind I struggled quickly to my feet. Hell, I almost fell for it!

I jammed my hands into my sleeves and pushed on, fighting the urge to run.

It was an eternity. I remember telling myself, chanting, push, Crabbe, push. Don't quit after all this. I also remember praying, sort of, to Mary, to help me just this one last time.

It was right after that I broke through the ice and crashed shin deep into water that was so cold it seemed to burn. I was so excited I shouted, "I've made it!" in words that were immediately whipped away by the wind. I now knew I was at the mouth of that shallow river that I'd floated down at the very start of my journey, the one with the sandbar. On I charged, exhilarated, breaking through ice all the way across the river and stumbling up the bank. In minutes I reached a cabin that was, luckily, unlocked.

With wooden hands I clumsily unlatched and pushed open the door. It took ages to fish my matches out of my pocket and to light one, since I could barely hold the box.

In the dim light I saw a coal-oil stove, bunk, sink, dresser. With the help of a second match I found a stub of candle. The thin linoleum crackled with the cold as I worked to get the stove alight. In no time the small cabin began to feel the effects of the stove.

Then I stripped off my outer clothing, letting it drop and stay where it fell. After drying my feet on a blanket, I dragged the bunk closer to the stove and climbed in.

I'm sure I smiled before I began to doze.

But the smile didn't last long. Pain would not allow me to fall into sleep, burning pain in my hands, feet and face. I knew that was the frostbite withdrawing and that there was nothing to do but wait it out. I climbed out of the bunk after a few hours of half-sleep and turned the stove down. The room was stifling by now, the windows fogged.

It was daylight—past noon by the look of the bright sun. Outside the cabin was a fantastically bright world of white. It hurt my eyes to look at it. And, incredibly, melted snow dripped off the eaves of the cabin.

I was still very weak, my legs shaky and my head light. It hurt to walk but I was parched so I found some old enamelled pots under the sink and set about melting snow. I drank and drank, coughing all the time: the warm liquid set me off. My chest hurt deep down.

I lay on the cot again, soaking in the warmth, the beautiful warmth. I could almost touch it.

I continued to doze. By the end of the day my face and feet were okay. My right hand was much better too, a bit stiff but clearly fine. My left hand was in deep trouble, though. The pinky and ring fingers were swollen up like ugly, yellow-brown sausages and the skin had begun to split. Anything that touched them set off ragged waves of pain throughout the hand and up my arm. When I made tea (dusty brown stuff I found on a shelf) and hung my clothes by the stove it was nip and tuck, one-handed fumbling.

The other thing that worried me was my chest. It was still sore and hurt like hell when I coughed.

The next morning I pulled on my clothes and shut off the stove. Since I had no mitts I tore strips from one of the wool blankets and wrapped my hands—clumsy but all right. The left I wrapped especially carefully until it looked like I was carrying a huge red club.

It was tough going to the main road: the snow was wetter with the warmer weather and hard to slug through. I began to hitch-hike and saw my first car pretty soon. It swooshed past, throwing up a great cloud of snow. Shortly afterward a bright, clean pick-up stopped for me. The driver had to lean across and open the cab door for me as I fumbled at the outside handle with my blanketed hand. With difficulty I clambered up and shut the door.

"Gotta put on yer belt before I take off," said the driver. He was a big, heavy guy, dressed in a red and green checkered bush shirt, denim overalls, and a wool hunting cap. He was friendly-looking, with fat cheeks and a W.C. Fields nose. It seemed strange to hear his voice—the only friendly human, other than Mary, I had heard in months.

I struggled with the seat-belt buckle for a bit and he leaned over to help, after slamming the gear-shift lever into Park.

"Some blizzard, eh?" he said as he drove off. "Heard on the news this morning it was the worst in twenty years."

"Yeah," I answered. "Pretty bad."

"We got the roads ploughed, though. Worked all last night. I drive a plough."

"Oh," I said.

He kept looking over at me.

"Somepin wrong with yer hand?" he asked.

"Yeah, frozen I think," I said, trying not to sound dramatic.

"Better have a look," he said as he pulled the truck over to the roadside. "Don't want to fool around with frozen fingers."

I couldn't unwrap it so he did.

"Jesus Christ!" he exclaimed when he saw the two yellowy fingers. "What happened? That's BAD!"

His eyes were bugging out of his face. Before I could answer he said excitedly, "We gotta get you to a doctor!" He rammed the truck into gear and tore away, fishtailing on the slippery road. Soon we were speeding along, slipping and sliding. I had visions of being wrapped around a tree in a metal envelope, or buried forever in the huge banks of snow that lined the road.

"Don't worry," my good Samaritan almost shouted, "you'll be okay."

I didn't feel okay. I was coughing like mad, every cough a sharp jab, but he was the only excited person in that pick-up.

He reached over his head and flipped a switch, then unclipped a hand mike. He said a stream of stuff into the thing, but I couldn't understand the weird mixture of words and numbers. I recognized "Ten-four" from T.V. shows, though. I wondered if he was really serious when he called the doctor a "sawbones."

We ripped into town at a furious pace, ran a red light, barrelled past a big stone church and pulled around a corner—slid is the proper word—onto a side street lined with spruce and stopped in front of a big rambling frame house with a wide verandah. A sign hung over the steps. My chauffeur jumped out, slammed the door, and ran up the steps.

He came back, hiked his portly body into the cab, made a skidding U-turn and got back on the C.B. as we tore through town. Hanging up the mike, he explained that the "Doc" was at the clinic, about a hundred miles south in Huntington. That's where we were going.

"Don't worry, Kid. I'll getcha there," he added confidently in a kind voice.

"Don't hurry on my account," I said weakly, hoping to slow this headlong flight.

"Gotta make tracks," he answered. "Can't fool around with frozen fingers."

We were on the highway now and the motion made me drowsy. I dozed a little.

I awoke to find myself being carried by that hulking character through sliding glass doors and down a long hall. I was so weak I didn't protest. I looked into his round face. You know, the guy really looked concerned. About a stranger.

He took me into a big room and laid me on a table. "Thanks," I murmured as he stepped out of sight.

Three women in white stood around me and one began to unwrap my hand. One gave orders in a quiet voice. When my hand was unwrapped they all went silent, but only for a minute.

Then I felt a needle.

Crabbe's Journal: 21

I woke up in a bed and my head hurt. So did my hand. So did my chest. I seemed to be in a white cell, under a high white ceiling lit with fluorescent lamps. Noises intruded slowly: coughing, slippered feet dragging on the floor, quiet voices.

The wall to the right of my bed began to move and I saw that the wall was a curtain hung on a track around my bed. It made a hissing noise as it moved away.

A face appeared above me, then disappeared. There was a needle in my right forearm and from it ran a clear tube to a bottle hung upside down on a rack beside my bed.

It was warm. I began to slip off again but the top half of the bed began to move, lifting me almost to a sitting position. I was in a dimly lit ward of about six beds, all of them occupied, it looked like. A woman in white pants and coat came over to the bed. I recognized her as the one who gave the orders in the other room.

"Hello. I'm Dr. Bruster. How are you feeling?"

"Lousy."

"Are you fully awake? I want to get some information

168

from you, but if you're too tired I'll come back. The anesthetic may not be fully worn off."

"The what? What happened?"

"Be easy. One step at a time." She took a pen out of her coat pocket, preparing to write on the chart she held clipped to an aluminum holder. She was small and skinny with vivid red hair cut short. The hair and steel-framed glasses made her look very business-like.

"What's your name?" she asked, her pen poised.

"Never mind."

"I beg your pardon?"

"I don't want to tell you."

She looked confused, her knitted brows bringing a harsh line to her face.

"Don't you want your family to know where you are?"

"You might say I don't have a family."

"Oh, I see." No, she didn't, but I let that pass.

"What's wrong with me? Why am I here?" I asked her.

She sidestepped that and tried a new tack.

"Are you still in pain?" The harsh line disappeared.

"I sure am." I was too. "My head, hand, chest."

She turned and mumbled something to the nurse who had just arrived. The nurse walked off again.

"All right, Mr. Stranger, it's like this." Her voice wasn't unkind. "You want it straight?"

I swallowed. My throat was dry.

"Of course."

"Your head hurts from the anesthetic. It will feel better soon. Your lungs hurt because you have a moderately seri-

---

ous case of double pneumonia. We thought there might be frost damage in there but so far the X-rays don't show anything."

The nurse had returned pushing a little cart with a tray on top. I saw a bottle of clear fluid and a needle.

"Your left hand," continued the doctor, "hurts from the operation. Luckily for you, and thanks to Jack Johnson, the man who drove you here, we were able to save your hand."

I lifted my aching, bandaged hand off the bed and looked at it for the first time.

"But," she went on, "we had to amputate the two damaged fingers."

"Jesus Christ!" I shouted. "You *what*?"

"Take it easy, son," she said softly. "Take it easy."

I gulped. Looking at the bandaged hand, you'd never know something was missing. I was shocked, but not surprised, if you know what I mean. The hand had looked awfully bad back in the cabin. I lowered the hand, afraid to think about what a horrible mess must be under the bandages. Strangely, it felt no different, just sore.

"I know it's hard, son," said the doctor. "But you almost lost the whole hand. Be thankful for that." I said nothing, still dazed by the news.

"We're sending you to the city, to a big hospital. You'll get a free ride all the way in an ambulance. Maybe they can find out who you are."

She turned to the tray and picked up the needle. She inserted it into the little bottle.

"But why?" I said.

"We don't have room enough for you here. This is a very small clinic. Now, I'm going to sedate you so the trip will be easier on you."

She leaned over, swabbed my arm and before I could say "Boo" I felt the stab and then nothing.

The next few days—maybe four or so, it's hard to keep track when you're drugged up—were mostly given to sleeping, getting needles, holding mediciny-tasting thermometers under my tongue, and having an icy stethoscope stuck under the funny nightshirt that tied down the back. I was sort of aware of being in a ward again but was so tired and groggy I didn't pay much attention.

As soon as I started feeling better they started coming after me about who I was: first a nurse, then a head nurse, then a doctor, then a stuffy-looking guy in a three-piece suit, an administrator, I guessed. He tried threats, then the cops.

The day nurse, a skinny, gray-haired but kindly woman whose white uniform hung on her like a rag, got me up on the sixth morning and led me out of the ward, down an antiseptic smelling hallway to a small, corner office. Mr. Three-piece, a bony, lanky type with thinning black hair and gold wire glasses, sat behind a polished wooden desk. Standing before the window, looking out, was a big man in a black leather car coat. Through the window I could see a bright sky and snow powder whipped into crazy patterns by the wind. When the nurse and I came into the room the big guy turned around.

"Thank you, Nurse Owens," said Three-piece. The door closed quietly.

"Sit down, young man," he said to me.

"No thanks. I'll stand." Since we were out of the ward I got the pipe out of the deep pocket of my bathrobe and began filling it.

Three-piece reacted quickly. "No smoking, if you don't mind."

"What about him?" I said, pointing the stem of the pipe at the big guy, who had a cigar sticking out of a round, friendly face. I wasn't sure, but I think I saw a shadow of a smile cross his features.

"He is a police officer. And an adult," answered the official from behind the desk. "I may be old fashioned, but I see no reason why your elders need follow the same rules as you."

Three-piece looked offended as the big guy blew a great cloud of acrid smoke into the room. He was enjoying this. I kept packing the bowl—a difficult job with one hand bandaged.

"Well, I don't know 'bout you but I gotta get a load off my feet." This from the big guy as he lowered himself into an imitation leather armchair and leaned forward, resting thick forearms on his legs. From that position he couldn't crane his neck enough to see me so he talked to the floor.

"You got any objection to telling me your name?" he said casually to the carpet.

"Yes." It seemed stupid to talk at the guy's balding head so I sat down, immediately realizing I'd been tricked. I took some time lighting up.

He straightened up, took a long haul of the cigar and shot the smoke out in a jet stream toward Three-piece, and crossed his arms over his wide chest. The leather coat creaked.

"Why?" came from behind the cigar.

I was stunned, because I couldn't think of an answer. You know how you get into a habit of thought and you forget why you think that way? I'd been secretive so long it was automatic. I'd had no time to think about my situation too much and his simple question broke through the habit of the last few months. Really, I thought at that moment, there was no point in hiding my identity any more. I felt a little dumb, as a matter of fact.

"Crabbe," I said. "Franklin Crabbe."

The cop smiled. Three-piece looked triumphant.

"Now we're getting somewhere!" he crowed, picking up his pencil. You could tell he had been going nuts because of all the empty blanks in the chart in front of him. Well, one blank filled, two thousand to go.

"Where ya from, Franklin?" said the cop.

I took the pipe out of my mouth.

"Crabbe. Don't call me Franklin."

The cop held up his beefy hands, palms toward me, and smiled again.

"Whatever you say, Crabbe."

I told him my parents' address, adding that I didn't live there any more. Three-piece looked over at the cop, impressed with the officer, and buttoned up his jacket before filling in some more blanks.

"Now," continued the policeman, "ya wanna fill me in on why you were found out in the middle of nowhere?"

"No," I said. "That's all you get."

Three-piece looked up, his face reddening. He pointed his pencil at me.

"Now you just listen, Mister"—at least I had graduated from young man—"we have to know the circumstances of your injuries and we have to know now, so stop all this childish nonsense."

Pleased with his cutting tone, he prepared to write. "Mind your own goddam business," I said evenly and stood up.

As I fumbled with the doorknob, the cop said, "I'm gonna bring your parents over here. I have to."

"If you have to do it," I said on my way out, "do it."

Digression

The thing I noticed when I was pretty young is that people have no imagination. I don't mean the kind of imagination you need to watch T.V. or read a book and go along with the story. I mean the kind of imagination you need to tolerate something different. To most people, if things don't fit their mental framework there must be something wrong with the *things*. Everything that doesn't conform is strange or crazy or "sick."

Take most teachers: they just can't accept you if you won't go along with the system. Oh, they have fancy words like "behavioral problem"—I've overheard *that* one a million times!—but in fact that kind of language is a cover for their lack of imagination. I knew lots of kids during my four years at high school who were independent. They made up their own minds about what they considered important and went their own ways. When their own way crossed the path of a teacher or got them at cross purposes with the system, everybody figured they were "problem." students. Nobody accepted the kids' right to set their own values. So the teachers came down on them. And that only made them more rebellious.

I always envied those kids, I guess because I decided years earlier to play the game. People like you to play the game, even if you cheat. They almost expect that. What they don't like is someone who refuses to play.

The cheater is accepted; the spoil-sport is considered to have "something wrong with him."

The students are worse than the teachers. Anyone or anything is either in or out with them. If you're out, you're considered insane and fair game for all sorts of attack and abuse. They're like a wolf-pack, snarling and snapping at everything "alien."

For instance, we had this teacher at my school who was very kind and harmless, but very different. For one thing, he refused to drive a car, or to own one. Called them landscape eaters. He rode an old, beat-up Raleigh to school. For another thing, he was a vegetarian. Every once in a while one of the kids would get him going by asking him why he didn't eat meat or drink alcohol. Because he was very naive (this caused more viciousness from the kids than any other characteristic—you always had to be in the know) he would stop whatever we were doing—irregular Latin verbs or something equally thrilling—and jam his hands into his jacket pockets and head off on a sermon about the wonderfulness of eating no meat. The poor guy really thought we were interested.

Can you imagine what they thought of him? All those dynamos fuelled with greasy hamburgers and barbecued steaks, who'd sell their souls for a slab of gooey pizza, a box of warm beer, or a tear around town on Friday night in the Old Man's Buick? They called him "The Veg" in honor of his eating habits and as a comment on his mind. They were certain a man like that must be crazy.

Well, I ran into that crap at the hospital too. Somebody decided I must be off-balance. I could just see Mr. Three-piece yakking about hostility and repressed whatnot. (I read some psychology last year.) That's how I got set up with Dr. Browne. I guess when *he* found out I was a person with a Mysterious Past he was overjoyed. And when he "dropped by" one afternoon, in the middle of a checker game I was having with this old guy in my ward, he "Hummed" every three seconds and raised his bushy little eyebrows every two.

What a find I must have been! Added to the pneumonia and mangled hand were a strange attachment to a pipe and a vivid red scar on the right wrist. But I wasn't going to end up in some boring article in a psych magazine. Not on your life.

Crabbe's Journal: 22

The cop brought my parents in a few days later. Nurse Owens got the honor of leading the prodigal son down another hallway, through a couple of sets of swinging doors, to a single door with "Lounge" painted on it in very unloungelike letters.

I stopped just before Mrs. Owens reached for the door handle.

"Wait," I said. "I don't want to go in yet."

She turned to look at me, searchingly, right into my eyes. I thought I caught an understanding flicker in hers. She walked back the way we had come, her loose uniform sort of floating on those skinny old bones of hers.

I stepped up and looked through the small pane in the door. My parents were standing in the middle of the empty lounge, close together, not talking, surrounded by chairs and sofas covered in cheap, pastel plastic. Harsh morning light splashed in through the panoramic window, filling the room with a white glare. Outside the wind shook the trees that stood in lonely rows.

My mother had on her full-length mink, as usual, but

something looked wrong. My eyes were drawn to her thin legs. They were bare. And on her feet she had a pair of old, scuffed chestnut penny loafers that she wore around home when she was puttering around the garden, tying and clipping the roses, on those rare moments when she seemed relaxed. But here she was wearing them *in public,* with her mink: this woman who wouldn't answer the door to pay the paperboy unless she was made up and dressed like a rich dowager from a lost empire or something.

When I thought that unkind thought my eyes rose to her face. The hard light from the window was not kind. She looked—old: skin tight over her cheekbones and sharp nose but a bit loose under her chin, wrinkles around her tired blue eyes. She was pale and worn. There was no joy in that tight, rigid face.

My father had on one of his dark, pinstriped lawyer suits, not quite so well pressed as usual, a bit wrinkled in fact. He was a little heavier around the middle now, a little greyer around the top. My father has a round, healthy-looking face, with large brown eyes and a wide, thin-lipped mouth that made him look friendly but tough. This day, he looked simply careworn and old.

You know, I never thought of my parents as people who would get old. But as I saw them looking so isolated standing together in the middle of that room, my father with his arm around my mother's thin shoulders, staring out the window, they became, suddenly, *people* to me—people getting older, looking worn and beaten down at this moment. What was going through their minds? I wondered. Why had my mother faced the world in such a state, bare-faced, bare-legged, in a mink and gardening shoes?

"What a son of a bitch you are, Crabbe. What a son of a bitch," I said under my breath, "to bring them to this." Tears streamed from my selfish eyes over my selfish face. I sobbed, my fists clenched in shame. I wept for the guilt I had caused them to feel.

I couldn't face them, drowned in shame. I turned and headed quickly down the hall, bursting through the first set of double doors.

"Stop, Crabbe." It was Mrs. Owens. She stood in the hall blocking my path. Quickly I wiped my eyes.

"Let me by," I spluttered, my voice cracked, childish.

"No," she said gently, "You have to go back. You have to. You have to tell them it's not their fault."

"But it is, dammit." I shot back, shouting. "It is their bloody fault."

A young nurse with a bundle of laundry in her arms was approaching us. She looked aside and scurried past.

Mrs. Owens said nothing as she took my rigid arm in her skinny hand and turned me around. She began walking me back slowly.

"You don't think that. If you did you'd not be crying, Crabbe. Those tears are your guilt and it's grief speaking to you."

I stopped, pulling my arm free as my anger flared. "What do you know about it?" I snapped, immediately regretting my outburst.

"I'm sorry," I said quickly. "I didn't mean that."

"'Course you didn't," she replied. She began to shepherd me along again. "You're not such a bad young fellow, you know," she said. "These old eyes of mine see more than you think. I've watched you in the few days you've been here, playing checkers with those old fellows that nobody wants to bother with, that nobody visits but maybe on a Sunday; running to the tuck shop for them on errands. Oh, you're not perfect, by any means. You can be nasty if it pleases you. To yourself most of all."

She was probably remembering the time I bit her head off because she wanted to get me back to bed and take my temperature when I was in the middle of a conversation about canoes with Old Ed, who lived in the bed directly across from mine. I realized later that it was *Ed* she wanted to rest.

"But you've something inside you," Mrs. Owens continued as we walked slowly along the hall toward the lounge, "that has to get itself born soon. I've raised five kids, Crabbe, three of 'em boys, and I know the signs. If you want to be a man you've got to get things straight between your parents and yourself first."

"Yeah, be a man," I said bitterly. "You sound like my father."

We stopped. She turned to me, dropping her arm.

"Well, yes, there's a lot of nonsense mixed up with that idea, to be sure. But it's not such bad advice, you know. You do have to learn to be a man. You must decide what being a man means to you, and you needn't take your Dad's definition by any means."

Mrs. Owens paused and looked right straight into my eyes, crossing her thin arms on her chest.

"You see, young man, it's like you were a seed and there's new life inside the shell, and it has to break the shell to get out. And when the shell splits from the force, well, that's a confusing and hurtful time. It's different for all of us, but we must all break free."

She took me by the shoulders, turned me to face the door and said, "Now, it's time to go and do what must be done."

I could hear her walking away down the hall in the opposite direction as I stood there facing the door. I knew if I wanted to, I could scratch the whole idea, never see them, go away as soon as I got out of the hospital. After all, I had no legal reason to see them again.

But all that was just excuse-making. I had to go in. I owed it to them. And to myself.

Crabbe's Journal: 23

All that stuff in the T.V. shows and soapy novels—you know, the long lost son rushing joyfully into his parents' forgiving arms, honey and syrup dripping all over them—is strictly nonsense. When I walked into the room and shut the door behind me and stood there, the lounge filled with sharp tension. They turned and looked at me, my Father's arm slipping from my Mother's shoulder. She had a lace hanky in her hand, all wrinkled and damp, and she began to worry it with her fingers.

Nobody spoke. I walked over and stood before them in the center of the room.

"Hi," I said, immediately feeling stupid at the emptiness of the greeting. "Let's sit down." I sat immediately in an armchair so nobody would fumble around, not knowing whether to hand out hugs or handshakes.

They took the couch opposite me. There was about eight feet of ugly worn beige carpet between us.

Silence again. My mother blew her nose. She kept looking at me, then away, like you do at a party when you want to check out a stranger but you don't want to seem obvious about it. My father unbuttoned his coat and looked at the floor.

"How have you been?" he said after clearing his throat noisily.

"I'm okay, now, thanks," I answered. "I'll be leaving in a couple of days."

"No, Dr. Browne says you should stay for another week," he said. "I think—"

"I'm all right, really," I cut in. "I'll leave when I think I'm ready."

"Now listen Franklin—" The old look I knew so well had invaded his face, so I cut off what I knew was going to be an order.

"Dad, I'm sorry to interrupt. Let's not start like this, okay?"

He accepted that and settled back into the sofa, crossing his ankles, an old habit. The plastic covering squeaked under his weight.

Silence again.

My mother continued to twist her hanky around and around her thin hands.

"Will you..." she began. "Will you be coming home, then?"

This question was quite a statement. The very fact that she didn't *assume* I'd come back or that my father didn't demand it told me that things had changed. A breakthrough.

I realized then, looking at their uncomfortable postures and hesitant, almost embarrassed faces that they were as confused as *I* was. Who was this stranger who confronted them, puffing away on a little pipe, sick and bandaged? Was he crazy? as Dr. Browne had probably told them. Would he blow up in front of them or fall down in a fit?

Mary once told me that the person who cares least about a relationship controls it. I realized that, if I wanted to, I could control this situation. But I didn't want to. And I especially didn't want to hurt them any more, or get revenge, or any of that crap. I just wanted to be taken seriously. I thought about what Mrs. Owens had said and it fit exactly with Mary's advice. I was a different person than the one who left these two parents months (or was it centuries?) ago. I did not intend to go back.

"I don't know," I answered my mother. "I... maybe... I don't know what I want to do yet."

More silence.

"It's not too late to go back to school, Franklin," said my mother hopelessly, like she felt she ought to try at least once. "The university would probably accept you as a late registration. Your father could speak to them." She rushed on, "You could come home and..." She trailed off after looking at my face.

"No, Mom. That's out. Definitely. Besides, I missed my diploma. I didn't write the finals."

"They gave it to you on your term work. But you missed the scholarship," said my father bitterly.

"I don't care, Dad, I just don't."

He looked away, out the window. This was hard for him. He and my mother had had it all planned and I wrecked it.

"Mom and Dad," I began a new tack, remembering Mrs. Owens, "I want to say something and I'm not sure how to. I'm sorry I did this to you."

My mother began crying, silently.

"I just want you to know it wasn't your fault, my running away. I thought it was, but it wasn't. It isn't anybody's fault."

"Oh, Franklin," her voice cracked. "We were afraid you were dead. The police... We had to check all the hospitals ...the morgue..." She broke down. Then anger swept into her voice. "How could you? How could you do that to me?"

I said nothing. After a bit she calmed down again. She blew her nose.

My father shifted unseeing eyes from the window to the tattered arm of the sofa. He began to pick at a rip in the covering. I was shocked to see his chin trembling. A single tear rolled down his broad cheek and plopped onto his lapel, unnoticed.

"What was it?" he said in a cracked whisper. "Where did I go wrong? What did I do wrong?"

He turned toward me. I had never seen my father show grief before.

"Aw, Dad, don't," I pleaded. "What's the point? There's no use going back. Can't we just put it behind us?"

"What's the point? I'll tell you what's the point, Franklin." His voice was rising. "I want to know. I want to know what was so goddam terrible about the way you were brought up. You had everything! Brains—the smartest kid in the school—the best of everything—home, family, a promising career, a future...."

He sort of wound himself down, like my mother did. His anger subsided.

"Dad," I said as gently as I could, "I was a rich, spoiled, mixed up, semi-alcoholic teenager who couldn't find his ass with both hands."

"You can't blame that on us!" hissed my mother. "And you *weren't* an alcoholic."

"I'm *not* blaming it on you," I continued as calmly as I could. "Can't you see that? I'm not blaming anything on anybody."

"Franklin," said my father, "you haven't answered my question. I have to know. I'm sorry I jumped on you a minute ago. I understand you're not blaming us, but I have to know what went wrong. It's driving me crazy."

"Don't you know, Dad? Deep down inside, don't you know?" He turned to the window again. "I want to be taken seriously, Dad, to run my own life. I'm not invisible. All my life I've been locked into other people's expectations— yours, Mom's, my teachers'. Everybody wants me to live *their* lives. Where do *I* come in? Being wealthy, being smart, that doesn't make it easier, Dad, it makes it *harder*. People expect more from you and when you don't measure up, if you're just a normal kid, they figure you're letting down the side. Lots of kids at school hate me because my parents are rich and I don't need to study. You know," I was really rolling, but very calm, not angry. I just wanted them to understand. "If I did something *well*, it was considered natural because I was wealthy, but if I screwed up, then *I* got the credit for the screw up! And the craziest part was, all my life, people acted like I was king of the world, like I had life by the short hairs. But I was just a goddam *slave*."

I looked at my parents, and I said quietly and with feeling, "Well that's over now. My life belongs to me. If you can't accept that... Well, it doesn't matter if you accept it or not."

I sat back, exhausted. I had a coughing fit; my chest still hurt a bit.

My father turned to my mother and said, "I guess that's that."

She nodded.

Silence again. They both studied the carpet. They must have been warned not to ask about what I was doing during my absence or where I was, because they said nothing.

After a while, they left. As I walked back to the ward, I felt like you do when you tidy up a room that has been so messy it's been bugging you for a long time, and you look it over. It makes you feel a little better, putting your house in some sort of order.

Crabbe's Journal: End

I signed myself out a few days later, once I was sure the pneumonia had cleared up, and went home. I had nowhere else to go. Besides, I didn't like the way I had left things with my parents.

We all sort of co-existed in a tense atmosphere for a few weeks. After all, there were quite a few taboos between us, a lot of old shadows from the past to dodge. But they really tried, and because they did, I did.

One thing that was hard to get used to was living and sleeping in a building. It almost drove me nuts. I felt so *closed in* all the time. After months of living outside with no walls between your skin and the horizon, a ceiling a few feet from your head takes getting used to. I spent long hours lying on my bed in the weak winter sunshine reliving those work-filled days of summer and early fall. It's strange how the tang of woodsmoke hanging in the air or the glint of sunlight on waves can glide into your mind almost as real as the real thing.

I had some bad moments too, remembering Mary, with no one to share the sadness. I owed her a lot. Not only my life, but the way I was trying to live it. And I knew that in a way she was part of my self, and she would be long after I stopped remembering her. My mother brought me into this world but Mary got me ready to live in it.

Don't think I spent that whole winter moping around, though. Not on your life. After a month or so of doing nothing, the inactivity was starting to get to me, so I took up jogging to get some exercise and stay in shape. I also answered an ad in the newspaper and got a job at a sheet-metal plant across town that manufactures office equipment, shelves, and certain auto-body parts. It's a small factory. The interview for the job was interesting. The foreman, a muscular, middle-aged guy named Brighton, had a blown-up photo framed on his desk of a canoeist shooting white-water rapids. He was the canoeist. Before our interview really got rolling I asked him about the picture and we got talking about canoe trips and camping. Brighton job-shares with another man who skis, so each can take a few months off work during the season he likes. I think I got the job because of the photo.

I sweep floors, mop up the cafeteria, clean the washrooms—fascinating stuff like that. My parents aren't too happy about Crabbe the Scholar doing unskilled labor but I wanted money for clothes and so on. I also wanted to pay them something for room and board. It's not a thrilling job, but the money's good, so it'll do for now.

As soon as spring chased the snow away I put a pack together and hitch-hiked up to the Ithaca Camp neighborhood. It took a new battery that I bought in that little one-horse town up there and a lot of coaxing (and some swearing) but I got the station wagon going. You know, the one I hid in the bush. It coughed and sputtered at first, and it sort of waddled into town on almost flat tires, but soon it was purring along. I pumped up the tires, filled the gas tank, and drove around for a while.

Ithaca Camp was a buzz of activity so I stayed away from there. But I did take a walk along the route I had traveled in the snowstorm. I wanted to find the pack and canoe I had abandoned but both were gone. It was a nice day so I pushed through to the lake at the beginning of the portage and spent the night there for old time's sake. Next day I headed back to the city.

When I rolled into our driveway my parents almost croaked. They had been pretty good about badgering me with questions about where I had run off to last spring but when I turned up with the car it was too much for them.

That night, at the dinner table, I noticed something strange. My father had removed that silly brass candelabra. So I took that as a favorable omen and gave my parents a heavily edited version of what I've written in this journal. They weren't completely satisfied with what I told them because they knew I was leaving out a lot and they asked me quite a few questions that I glossed over or avoided altogether. And there was still some bitterness, theirs *and* mine, cooking away under the surface of our conversation, but nobody was lecturing anybody, and for the first time I was able to talk to them without the feeling that someone else had written our lines for us.

Not long after that, an interesting thing happened at work. I started jogging on my lunch hours and discovered that Brighton, the foreman, and I have something else in common: running for fitness. He does it to keep in shape for canoeing. So on days when he isn't too busy in the office, we run together.

You'd expect a guy like Brighton to be super-macho. But he isn't; he's actually a very gentle person. One day as we slogged through the grimy streets near the plant, he told me about an outfit he and his wife run in the summer. It's called Project Adventure and it's connected with Family Court. He and his wife take kids who have been in trouble with the law, and would ordinarily go to some kind of reform school, on wilderness canoe trips for two or three weeks at a time. The idea is to get them away from bad influences and, more important, help them grow some self-respect and cooperation with other people. "What the psychologists call 'social skills,'" he said.

I asked him if I could come along on one of the trips. I was dying to get back into the bush and I thought I'd like to work at something like that, where you do something good, or at least try to. Brighton says these kids don't like themselves too much. Maybe I could do for someone what Mary did for me, on a smaller scale of course.

So, in a couple of weeks I'm going on a canoe trip with the Brightons, and they're going to test me out and see if I can handle myself outdoors.

I'm pretty sure I can satisfy them.